DANGEROUS DIAMONDS

Other books by Barbara Mitchelhill

Storm Runners
Winner of the Solihull Children's Book Award
and shortlisted for the East Sussex Children's Book Award

DANGEROUS DIAMONDS

BARBARA MITCHELHILL

Andersen Press
London

First published in 2009 by
Andersen Press Limited
20 Vauxhall Bridge Road London SW1V 2SA
www.andersenpress.co.uk
www.barbaramitchelhill.com

Reprinted 2010

British Library Cataloguing in Publication Data available.

ISBN 978 184 270 978 8

Typeset in Garamond Three by Palimpsest Book Production Limited,
Grangemouth, Stirlingshire, FK3 8XG.

Printed and bound in Great Britain by CPI Bookmarque,
Croydon CR0 4TD

1
Not Hot Dogs

Edinburgh, Scotland

Harry Brodie was not usually suspicious but he couldn't help thinking there was something odd going on. Looking down into the Grassmarket earlier that morning, he had noticed a hot-dog van. It was a faded yellow and on the roof was stuck a huge plastic sausage which dribbled red plastic ketchup. Not the kind of van you would forget easily. It had been parked opposite the flat just after breakfast. Now it was half past eleven and it was still there. But it hadn't sold a thing. It hadn't moved. Neither had the two men inside.

Harry was sitting on the window seat, waiting for his sister to get ready. He pushed his glasses up his nose and stared down at the old cobbled road which was the Grassmarket. It was busy with traffic as usual and the large parking area down the middle was crammed with cars and motorbikes and the one hot-dog van.

He glanced at his watch and frowned. He had been

1

waiting for Charlie for ages. Why did she take forever to get ready? She had changed her mind a hundred times about what to wear. Should it be pink or purple? Should it be jeans or a skirt? Trainers? Boots? Flip-flops? Honestly! Did it matter? Who cared?

He got up and banged on her bedroom door. 'Get a move on, Charlie, or we'll miss the start of the show.'

No reply.

'Be like that, then,' he mumbled under his breath.

He walked down the hall to a white-painted door covered with coats and anoraks hanging on hooks. Harry pushed them aside and turned the handle. 'Dad,' he shouted up a narrow staircase. 'Have you finished? It's time we were off.'

From the study under the eaves came Dad's reply. 'Give me five minutes, Harry, and I'll be with you.'

But Harry knew that his five minutes could stretch to an hour. Dad had been up there since breakfast and when Harry had gone up to talk to him, he had seemed distracted. Not his usual self. Maybe he had a problem with his book. That was the trouble with writers. They dreamed a lot. They lived in another world.

Harry banged on his sister's door for the second time. 'CHARLOTTE!' he yelled. And when there was still no reply, he ran his fingers through his short, red hair and stormed back into the living room. There he slumped, exasperated, onto the window seat again. He pressed his freckled forehead against the glass, gazing down from the fourth-floor window into the road below trying to forget his impossible family and stared at the hot-dog van.

His eyes were still fixed on it when Charlotte burst into the room.

'How do I look, bro?' she said, twirling round with her arms spread wide to show off her short purple skirt, glitter jelly sandals and flower-strewn T-shirt.

Harry merely grunted and didn't take his eyes off the window.

'What you looking at?' Charlotte asked, leaning over his shoulder.

'Down there,' he said, nodding at the parking area. 'Two scruffy blokes have been sitting in that yellow van for hours.'

'So?' said Charlotte. 'They're selling hot dogs. What's the big deal?'

Harry turned and glowered. Was this dumb blonde really his twin or had she dropped in from outer space?

'Listen,' he said. 'I just saw some kids try to buy hot dogs and they were told to get lost. Anyway, the cab's fogged up with cigarette smoke. You're not supposed to smoke around food.'

Charlotte screwed up her face. 'Yuk! That is totally disgusting,' she said. 'It's a danger to health.'

She was explaining how she would send them to prison for ten years *at least* and feed them bread and water when Dad appeared in the doorway. 'I'm ready, kids,' he said. 'Shall we go?'

Charlotte whirled round. 'Dad!' she shrieked, pointing at his feet. 'You can't go to the theatre like that. You've got odd shoes on.'

It was true. One was black and one was a light tan colour. Even his socks were different. Charlotte sighed. This was the kind of thing Mum had mentioned before she left for the States. She had asked them to be sure and keep an eye on dippy old Dad. He could do such odd things sometimes – like putting dirty socks in the fridge or ice cream in the oven.

'Oh,' said Dad, looking down at his shoes. He grinned sheepishly. 'I'll go and get changed.'

Five minutes later, all three Brodies walked down the twisting stone stairs that led from the fourth floor to street level and the door of flat 41A. They stepped out into the Grassmarket and Harry slammed the door behind him.

Charlotte, wildly excited, ran ahead. 'I can't believe we're going to see Ricky Waters,' she squealed and raced across the road, arms in the air, ponytail flying. 'He's my *numero uno* favourite.'

There was a screech of brakes as a car narrowly avoided her. Harry squeezed his eyes shut and wondered, not for the first time, how someone like him could end up with a twin who did such crazy things. She didn't even look like him. She was as skinny as a washboard and dressed like a Barbie doll. He looked down at his jeans and trainers. At least one of us has taste, he thought.

When the traffic was clear, Harry and Dad crossed the road and as they walked through the parking area, Harry glanced across at the hot-dog van. The two men inside had slumped down in their seats. They had turned their faces away from him as if they didn't want to be seen. Why would they do that? They had been parked in the Grassmarket all morning. What were they waiting for? he wondered.

He couldn't help feeling that something was wrong.

2
A Good Show and a Bad End

They walked across town and by the time they reached Princes Street, the pavements were crowded with tourists up for the Edinburgh Festival. People everywhere, up for the summer holiday. Too many, thought Harry.

When they finally turned into George Street they saw there was a massive queue outside the Assembly Rooms where Ricky Waters was performing.

'Sure you've got the tickets?' Harry called to Dad, who was walking, hands in pockets, several paces behind them.

He looked up, tapping his jacket pocket. 'Sure,' he said. Then he glanced at his watch. 'But we've got five minutes before they open the doors. I want to make a phone call. You two go and stand in the queue. I won't be long.'

The twins joined the line outside the Assembly Rooms and waited. When Dad returned, Harry saw he looked tense. Very tense.

'You OK, Dad?' he said.

Dad shook his head. 'Can't get a signal. I'll try again later.'

Harry slapped him on the back. 'Chill out, Dad. The show's going to be great.' And Dad attempted to smile.

At last, the queue of people began to move forward and the Brodies followed, shuffling towards the marble-floored entrance hall and up the grand staircase of the magnificent old building and into the theatre.

Charlotte – bossy as ever – organized them in their seats and passed round a bag of sweets before the lights went down and the buzz of the audience fell silent. They sank back in their seats as a spotlight lit the empty stage and the small, skinny shape of Ricky Waters appeared from the wings and waddled up to the microphone.

For the next hour they listened to silly jokes and rocked with laughter. At one point Charlotte fell off her seat and Harry had to yank her up again. They laughed so much that they ached and were left gasping for air.

'That was so cool,' Harry said, as they stood up to leave. 'He's even funnier on stage.'

'I nearly burst laughing,' said Charlotte. 'What do you think, Dad? Wasn't he great?'

Dad nodded. 'Very good,' he said but it was obvious to Harry that he was far away again. Why couldn't writers be normal? he thought.

They walked out of the theatre, jostling with the raucous audience on the stairs. Halfway down, Charlotte leaned over the banister rails and pointed into the foyer. 'They're selling ice cream, Dad. Can we have one?'

At the bottom of the staircase, Dad reached into his pocket and handed Charlotte a note. 'Go and get your ice creams while I try to make that call again. Meet you back here in five minutes.'

Flicking open his mobile, Dad walked out into George Street while the twins pushed their way through the crowd, to the ice-cream seller. Another queue. Five minutes at least. Oh well, thought Harry, there's time to choose which ice cream to buy. In the end, he had Fudge Ripple and Charlotte had Strawberry Whip with chocolate sprinkles, which is what she always had.

Licking their cones, they walked out onto the pavement to meet Dad. But it was crowded with people heading for the next show.

'Can you see him?' Charlotte asked as she stood on tiptoe.

'No,' said Harry and walked a few steps along the road, looking one way and then the other.

'Don't go wandering off, Harry,' Charlotte said. 'Stay by the doors so Dad can find us.'

Harry pulled a face at his sister before turning away. He couldn't help wondering why Dad was taking so long. 'How far does he have to go to get a signal?' he said. 'The North Pole? A phone call can't be that important.'

'Don't panic,' said Charlotte, finishing her Strawberry Whip. 'He might have gone into a book shop or some-thing. You know what he's like.'

Harry snorted and folded his arms across his chest. 'He's been in a right miserable mood all day. He's probably forgotten about us. I bet he's gone off home.'

They waited another half hour and when Dad still hadn't come back, Harry flipped. 'That's it!' he said taking a swinging kick at a waste bin. 'I'm off.'

And he set off to walk back to the flat with Charlotte hurrying behind.

When they arrived at 41A, he took his key from his pocket and unlocked the door.

'Good thing I've got my key,' he said. 'Or does Dad want us to spend hours waiting on the pavement?'

'Stop whingeing,' said Charlotte as they stepped

into the tiny hallway. 'If we'd taken our mobiles, Dad would have phoned us to explain.'

The Brodies' flat was at the top of an ancient, blackened building in one of the oldest parts of Edinburgh. The only way up was by a spiral staircase – thirty-eight stone steps worn thin in the middle over hundreds of years. When Harry was halfway up, he stopped. 'What's that smell?'

Charlotte sniffed. 'It's cigarettes.'

'But Dad doesn't smoke,' said Harry. 'Where's it coming from?'

He hurried on up the stairs. The smell was getting stronger. When he reached the top, he came to a sudden halt. He mouth fell open and his eyes grew wide as golf balls.

'Oh no!' he gasped. 'Look at this!'

Charlotte peered over his shoulder. The oak chest that stood in the hall had been overturned. Even the cupboard at the far end had been opened and its contents scattered over the carpet.

'We've been burgled,' said Harry. 'While we were at the show, somebody broke in!'

3
Who to Call?

Charlotte pushed past her brother. 'Harry, did you lock the door behind you when we went out? You were last.' She didn't wait for a reply. 'How many times has Dad told you? You always forget!'

'Don't yell at me!' Harry snapped. He glowered at his sister and stepped forward until they were nose to nose. 'Listen, I *did* lock it. I *remember*.'

Harry marched through the flat with Charlotte in tow, assessing the damage. The living room. The kitchen. The bedrooms. The whole place had been trashed.

'What about Dad's study?' Harry said.

'Of course,' said Charlotte and they hurried down the hall, opened the white-painted door and ran up the narrow flight of stairs.

Charlotte was first. 'It's absolutely fine! They haven't touched a thing. Why would they leave this room when they've ransacked everywhere else?'

Harry stood staring at Dad's desk with his laptop and the scanner and printer. Any self-respecting burglar would have taken them. But they had moved nothing.

'They didn't touch anything because they didn't come up here,' he said at last.

'Why not?'

'*We* know this room is here but I bet the burglars didn't. The door isn't easy to spot, is it?'

'I suppose it is pretty well covered with our anoraks and stuff,' said Charlotte. 'Mum's always saying the hooks will break off one day. The burglars wouldn't think there was a door behind all those coats.'

Harry stood chewing his bottom lip. 'They broke into the flat. They were obviously looking for something. But what? They've made a right mess but they haven't taken a thing.'

It wasn't as if Dad was rich, he thought. He was a writer who wrote thrillers and didn't earn a huge amount of money. Mum was an actress and she was out of work a lot of the time. So there were no antiques or state-of-the-art TVs or valuable jewellery. Yet Dad's camera was in the bedroom and they hadn't even taken that. Harry shook his head, unable to make sense of it.

'I think we'd better tell the police,' he said.

But Charlotte disagreed. 'No. Let's ring Mum.'

'What could she do? She's in the States. No point in getting her upset, is there?' Harry went over to the desk and picked up the phone. 'I'm ringing the police. I'll tell them somebody broke in.'

Before he could dial the number, Charlotte snatched the phone out of his hand. 'That's stupid, Harry. You know what they'll say.'

'What?'

'They'll say, "Where's your father? Oh dear, we can't leave you kids here by yourselves." Then Dad will get into trouble and they'll make a terrible fuss and send Social Services. Is that what you want?'

It was not what Harry wanted at all. He just wished his goofy dad had not gone wandering off without telling them.

'Right then,' he said. 'We'll go down and clear up a bit and wait for Dad to get back.'

But his head was bursting with questions. Why would anyone break into the flat? What were they looking for? In the last three weeks, Dad hadn't done anything unusual. He had been working hard on the last chapters of his book. He had been at home every day until they had gone to the show. So someone had been waiting until the flat was empty.

As Harry turned towards the stairs, he noticed

something scribbled on the white board on the wall and he went over to read it.

> ***IMPORTANT
> TUESDAY – *see Edina re cover – borrow artefact – something old and creepy?*
> – *ring Tom for photo session*
> DON'T FORGET

'What's this, Charlie? Did Dad go out yesterday?'

'Dunno. I went shopping with Fiona.'

'And I was at tae kwon do.'

'Then he could have done and we wouldn't know,' said Charlotte. 'What's that got to do with anything?'

'If he borrowed something from the museum, it might have been valuable, that's all. Just a thought. The burglars could have taken that.'

'Mmm,' said Charlotte. 'You're dreaming, bro. It's not likely.'

'But why don't we ring Edina? At least we can tell her what's happened.'

Edina Ross was an old friend of Dad's. They had been at university together years ago and she had recently moved back to Edinburgh after travelling round the world. She'd taken a post in the Medieval

Department of the Museum of Scotland, which was just up the road. Edina was a will-o'-the-wisp, Dad said. She never stayed long anywhere – and that's probably why the twins found her exciting. She always had a story to tell.

Yes, they would ring Edina. She would know exactly what to do.

4

The Reliquary

A list of phone numbers that Dad often used was typed on a piece of paper and pinned to the wall. They found the one for the museum and dialled it.

'Medieval Churches Department, please,' said Charlotte to the receptionist and waited, expecting that the next voice she would hear would be Edina's. But she was wrong.

'Briony Calder speaking. How can I help you?'

'Oh,' said Charlotte, taken aback. 'We were hoping to speak to Miss Ross.'

'I'm afraid she's in London. She's been at a conference all week but she'll be back tomorrow. You can speak to her then.'

Charlotte stuttered. 'Oh, er . . .'

'Unless there's something I can help you with?' Miss Calder said.

Harry snatched the phone from his sister's hand. 'Hi. It's Harry Brodie speaking.'

'James Brodie's little boy?'

Harry cringed at her words. He was nearly thirteen

and hardly little. But he went on. 'Yes,' he said. 'We were interested in that thing that Dad borrowed yesterday.'

'The reliquary?'

'Er, yes, the er . . .'

'Reliquary.'

'Could you tell us something about it?' said Harry and then he added, 'It's for homework. History.'

Miss Calder gave a little twitter of laughter. 'Of course, my dear. I don't suppose your father knows a great deal about it. He just wanted it for the cover of his book, didn't he?'

'Yes,' said Harry. 'I suppose you've got quite a few of them.'

'We have one or two reliquaries. They're very old boxes – quite small, of course – sometimes made out of wood. But the one your father borrowed is rather beautiful, isn't it? That's made of silver and copper.'

'What were they used for?' asked Harry.

'Remains,' Miss Calder replied. 'They put small remains of saints inside. Locks of hair. Finger bones. That kind of thing.'

'Gruesome,' said Charlotte, who was standing with her ear as close as possible to the phone.

'And are they valuable?'

17

'Some are quite valuable,' said Miss Calder, who seemed to be enjoying their chat.

'How valuable?'

'It varies. A few hundred to a thousand or so.' She giggled a little. 'When your father called in yesterday, I was just opening a box of artefacts that had arrived that morning.' She chatted on. 'Your father was quite taken with the reliquary. He was going to get it photographed, he said. Of course I knew Miss Ross wouldn't mind. Your father is an old friend. That's right, isn't it?'

'Sure,' said Harry. 'They go way back.'

There was a pause on the line then Miss Calder spoke again as if she had remembered something. 'Harry,' she said. 'I wonder if I could speak to your father?'

Harry hesitated before answering. 'Sorry. He's out.'

'It's just that he said he would bring the reliquary back this afternoon. It's possible he's forgotten of course. I expect he's terribly busy.'

'Yes,' said Harry. 'But I expect he'll bring it tomorrow.'

'Of course,' said Miss Calder. 'I'm sure it's safe. Silly me. But perhaps you'd be kind enough to remind him when he comes home.'

And with that, they ended the conversation.

Harry put the receiver down and sank into Dad's office chair. 'So the burglar could have been looking for the reliquary,' he said. 'But I don't think he found it.'

'Obviously,' said Charlotte, pointing to a shelf over the filing cabinet. 'I think that's it.'

There among a collection of pens and Sellotape and a pile of papers was a small box made of silver and copper – exactly as Miss Calder had described it.

Charlotte reached up and took it off the shelf. 'It's tiny,' she gasped. 'They couldn't have been looking for this, could they?'

They stood staring at the box in her hands. It was no more than ten centimetres long and four wide – a rectangular box with a lid shaped like the roof of a house. It was made of wood and plated in silver which had tarnished long ago. Tubes of copper had been fixed on every edge and copper discs decorated the sides. It looked very old. Several hundred years, they guessed.

Charlotte's stomach fluttered nervously as she wondered what was inside. Would there be finger bones? Or hair pulled from a saint's head? Yuk! She placed her hand on the lid and gripped it with her fingers, daring herself to open it. But she couldn't. No. She daren't.

'Let me have a look,' said Harry, impatient to see

what was inside. And when he opened it up, he found nothing. It was empty except for a bit of dust and grime. 'No bones,' he said. 'Nothing spooky. Shame.'

'Of course, I knew that,' said Charlotte and tried to snatch it out of Harry's hands. 'Let me see. Let me. Let me . . .' In the tussle that followed, the reliquary slipped through Harry's fingers and crashed to the floor.

As it fell, part of it, the bottom of the box, came loose and something spilled out. Spread over the bedroom carpet, they saw a group of small, shining diamonds – thirty or forty of them – looking like tiny splinters of glass, glinting in the shaft of sunlight that beamed through the window. They were beautiful.

The Brodie twins stared at the diamonds and their mouths fell open.

5
Diamonds Are Forever

Charlotte let out a long low whistle. 'Awesome!' she said, twisting her ponytail round her finger and grinning. 'You'd have to be a famous footballer to afford that lot. I bet they'd have diamond earrings made for their girlfriends or maybe fantastic rings.'

Harry sighed. Trust his sister to think about stuff like that. While she went off into fantasy land, it was left to him to think what they should do next. As usual, he thought.

'We'll have to go to the police,' he said, bending down and putting some diamonds onto the palm of his hand. 'These are worth a fortune.'

Charlotte raised her eyebrows and shook her head. 'No way! Use your brains, bro. If Dad knew the diamonds were there, why didn't he go to the police? If we tell them, we might get him into terrible trouble.'

Harry snapped back. 'If you think he put them in the reliquary, you're crazy.'

'I'm not crazy,' said Charlotte. 'And I don't believe

Dad's involved in anything crooked. But we should wait till he comes back. If he thinks he should call the police, then let him do it.'

They crouched down and picked up all the diamonds – thirty-two of them. Sparkling. Radiating colours from their facets like tiny stars. One by one, they put them back into the false bottom in the reliquary, where they had been hidden. They sealed them over again and shut the lid.

Charlotte glanced up at Harry. She suddenly looked pale and anxious. 'I didn't think,' she said, hesitating nervously. 'Well . . . It's only just occurred to me . . . What if Dad hasn't wandered off? What if he's had an accident?'

'Like what?'

'Been knocked down by a car or something.'

They hadn't thought about that. They had been so angry with him. Thinking he had just forgotten about them. Dippy as usual. They had marched off without wondering if something had happened to him. Once they were back home and confronted with the shock of the burglary, they hadn't thought about anything else.

They decided to ring the hospital. It didn't take long. When they explained their worries to the receptionist at the other end, they were put through to Accident and Emergency straightaway. They gave Dad's name and a description – a man in his forties, tall, dark hair and dressed in jeans and a blue sweater. But no one of that description had been brought in that afternoon. Dad was definitely not at the hospital.

'Right,' said Charlotte. 'If he isn't back in an hour, how about trying Edina's mobile? We've got to talk to somebody.'

'Do you know her number?' asked Harry.

'It's on the list,' said Charlotte, pointing to the piece of paper pinned to the wall.

'OK,' said Harry. 'One hour. Then we phone her.'

To pass the time, they cleared up the mess that the burglar had left behind and, by late in the afternoon, Dad had still not returned and had not phoned. So Charlotte dialled Edina Ross's mobile.

She answered in her businesslike voice. 'Edina Ross.'

'Hello, Edina. It's Charlotte Brodie here.'

'Charlotte! How lovely to hear from you. I've just this minute walked into the house. I've been in London all week.'

'You're home?'

'Yes and I'm exhausted. My train was late and I'm very hungry. Now, what can I do for you?'

'I had to ring because Harry and I are in real trouble.'

Charlotte kept the conversation brief. She knew from watching thrillers on TV that it was easy to tap into phone lines. Best to say as little as possible.

'Can we come round?' she asked. 'We need someone to talk to. Is that all right?'

'Of course you can,' Edina said. 'I'm always happy to see you two. You know that.'

'Can we come straightaway?'

'Of course. And I'll see if there's any of Mrs McFee's chocolate cake. You head straight over here and tell me what's worrying you.'

Charlotte put the phone down and turned to Harry. 'She says we can go round.'

'Let's go then,' he said.

But Charlotte stood still, biting on a fingernail. 'Do we take the reliquary with us? What if we get robbed?'

Harry was already in the hall pulling on his anorak. 'Of course we take it. We need to show her what we found. Anyway, it belongs to the museum and she works there.'

'But what about the diamonds?' Charlotte said as she hurried down the hall to the row of coat hooks. 'Why don't we hide them in the freezer? You know – put them with the ice cubes so nobody would see them.' She reached for her red satin jacket, the one with *Girl Power* printed in silver on the back, and pulled it on. 'I saw that idea once in a film. It was brilliant.'

Harry sighed a four-star sigh and gave her one of his funny looks. 'No, Charlie. We'll take them to show Edina.'

Charlotte shrugged and walked into the kitchen where she wrote a note for Dad and left it propped up on the table.

Dear Dad,
We've gone to see Edina. Please ring us.
Love,
Charlotte and Harry XXXXXX

He might come back while we are out, she thought. I hope. I hope. I hope.

6
Chocolate Cake

They strapped on their helmets and checked their mobiles were in their pockets before pulling their bikes from the space behind the front door.

With the reliquary safely in Harry's saddlebag, they set off down the Grassmarket towards King's Stables Road and in less than half an hour, they had reached Dean Terrace where Edina lived.

Usually they met her at the museum but they had been here once with Dad, soon after she moved in. Her house was in the middle of the long row of grand Edwardian houses overlooking a wooded bank that dropped down to the river. Edina's house had four storeys with a basement beneath and was seriously big.

'She must have plenty of dosh,' Harry said, looking up at the elegant stone façade. 'Loads more than Dad or Mum.'

Charlotte nodded. 'Yep. You need mega bucks to own a big place like this. One or two famous people live round here, you know. I've read about them in a celeb mag.'

Harry groaned, irritated by the fact that his sister was so keen on rubbish magazines. Why couldn't she think about something more interesting? Like tae kwan do.

They fastened their bikes to the iron railings before Harry took the reliquary from his saddlebag, wrapped in a plastic carrier. They walked up the steps to the black painted door and Charlotte grasped the lion's head knocker and struck it three times before they heard footsteps echoing down the hall. When the door opened, Edina was standing there with a broad, broad smile, her brown hair as wild and frizzy as always, and dangly earrings peeping through.

'Charlotte! Harry! Come in,' she said, hugging them both and covering them in a cloud of her perfume, which was much too heavy and cloying for their taste. 'I promised you chocolate cake,' she said, 'and you shall have some. Follow me.' And without pausing, she spun round and led them down the hall, her long, multi-coloured skirt swishing as she walked ahead.

'How about this?' she said with a sweep of her hand towards the kitchen table. There was a tray already laid with a plate of sandwiches and the biggest chocolate cake they had ever seen. 'OK?'

Harry and Charlotte grinned and nodded in appreciation.

'Then we'll go up to the sitting room so we can talk.' Edina picked up the tray and walked in front, her high heels clicking over the black and white tiles of the hall floor.

It is often the case that Edwardian houses have the sitting room on the first floor at the top of a grand flight of stairs. And this was so in Edina's house.

She slipped off her Jimmy Choos and carried the tray up the stairs.

'Leave your shoes at the bottom, kids, will you?' she called over her shoulder. 'Mrs McFee gets very cross if she has to get her scrubbing brush out.'

Charlotte dug Harry in the ribs and nodded towards his trainers. He shrugged and bent down to undo his laces while Charlotte kicked off her jelly sandals and left them on the tiles. Edina's carpets were such a pale shade of cream that the smallest mark would have shown.

The twins followed her up the stairs and into a large sitting room with two high windows, overlooking the trees across the street. Everything was immaculate. More cream carpets. Cream sofas. Cream curtains. All this, they thought, was nothing like their own home at 41A, which was filled with kids' stuff, some threadbare carpets and – they had to admit – four untidy people.

When they sat on the sofa opposite Edina, Harry tucked the carrier bag behind him, waiting until the time was right to show her the reliquary. Edina passed a plate of sandwiches from the tray she had set down on a large coffee table. 'I've just got back from London,' she said, 'and I met some very interesting people. Let me tell you about this millionaire who has a whole stable of horses and a helicopter . . .'

While they helped themselves to the food, Edina entertained them with stories of her trip. She could always make things sound like fun, Harry thought, as he bit into a slice of chocolate cake. She even looked quite interesting – not at all like his Barbie-doll sister. Just take that Egyptian ankh on the chain round her neck. Where did that come from? he wondered.

By the time they had eaten several sandwiches and a large slice of chocolate cake, Edina had come to the end of her stories. 'Now then,' she said. 'Your turn. What's all this about you wanting to talk to me?'

Harry reached behind him, pulled out the plastic bag and put it on the coffee table.

'What's this?' she asked.

He leaned forward and unwrapped the reliquary before passing it to Edina.

'It's from your museum,' he said. 'Dad borrowed it.'

Edina took it in her hands and examined it. 'This must be part of the new consignment,' she said, sinking back onto the sofa. 'It shouldn't have been lent out, really.'

'Is it valuable?' asked Harry.

'No, not terribly. We have reliquaries much more valuable than this one. I don't know why James chose it. It's not particularly attractive, is it? I'll take it back, if you like.' She looked at the twins, her brow furrowed with puzzlement. 'But why have you brought it? Why hasn't James come with you?'

'He doesn't know we've come,' Charlotte said as she got to her feet and took hold of the reliquary. 'Just wait till I show you this,' she said, fumbling inside. 'It's got a secret.' She took out the false bottom and held it out so Edina could see the diamonds.

Her face drained of colour. 'Oh, my goodness,' she said. 'Where have these come from?'

'That's what we want to know,' said Harry.

Then they told her the whole story of what had happened that afternoon – Dad going walkabout, the burglary and finding the diamonds.

'It's awful,' said Charlotte. 'We don't know what to do. That's why we had to talk to you.'

'Do you think we should call the police?' asked Harry. 'We're worried about Dad. We've checked with the hospital and he's not there.'

Edina set the reliquary down on the coffee table. She leaned forward and chewed on her finger as she tried to come up with an answer.

'I think it best,' she said eventually, 'if you wait for your father to come back. I expect he's gone off on one of his airy-fairy dreams – you know what he's like. After all, people just don't suddenly go missing. I expect he'll be home when you get back. Just you see.'

The twins felt better for hearing that and they relaxed.

Edina smiled. 'Anyway, contacting the police could make matters . . . er . . . complicated for your father. I think it better if you do nothing and tell no one.'

'That's what *I* thought,' said Charlotte, wrinkling her nose at Harry. 'But my brainy brother was all for going to the police.'

Before the conversation could break out into a full-blown argument, Edina cut two slices of gateau and insisted they ate them. With their mouths full, they couldn't quarrel.

'I think I should keep the reliquary here,' Edina said as they bit into the chocolate cake. 'I'll look after it until James comes back.'

'Sure,' said Charlotte, spitting crumbs. 'If you don't mind. That would be great.'

Edina got up, holding the reliquary to her chest. 'I'll take it up to my study,' she said. 'You sit and enjoy your cake. I won't be long.'

They heard her walk up another flight of stairs to the next floor and they felt relieved that the reliquary was now in safe hands.

7
Trust No One

They cycled home, hoping that Dad would be there when they got back but fearing that he wouldn't be.

As soon as they unlocked the door of 41A, they called up the stairs, 'Dad! Are you back?' But there was no reply. And the note that Charlotte had written was still on the kitchen table, untouched. But the red light was flashing on the answerphone.

'There's a message, Harry,' Charlotte squealed. 'It's Dad! I just know it's Dad.'

Harry was nearest and he pressed the play button.

'You have one message timed today at 16.35 pm. Message one . . .'

They held their breath while they waited to hear who had called.

'Hello, Mr Brodie. Briony Calder here from the museum.'

They sighed with disappointment as they recognized the voice.

'Miss Calder!' said Charlotte. 'Not Dad.'

As they listened to the message they became aware

of how nervous she sounded. This was not the bright, twittery woman they had talked to that afternoon.

'I'm so sorry to bother you,' she said, 'but I wonder if you could bring the reliquary back as soon as possible. Oh dear . . . I don't suppose you'll get this message before we close but anyway . . . Miss Ross has just telephoned and she's terribly upset. She tells me the reliquary is one of the most valuable things in the museum. I would never have let it go if I'd known. Well, you can understand how shocked I was and, frankly, Miss Ross is so angry with me I fear I'll lose my job. So . . . I was wondering . . . could you possibly return it first thing tomorrow . . . without fail . . . Please.'

The phone went dead.

'End of messages,' said the automated voice. 'To delete messages, press delete.'

The twins looked at each other in disbelief.

'Did she say "valuable"?' said Harry in a mocking tone. 'One of the most valuable things in the museum? What's she on about? Edina told us it wasn't worth much.'

Charlotte nodded. 'She said they had other reliquaries worth more. What's going on?'

They sat, elbows on the kitchen table, trying to work it out.

'The reliquary itself is not worth a fortune,' said

Harry, chewing on his lip. 'But with the diamonds inside, it certainly is.'

'I don't get it,' said Charlotte, spreading her arms wide. 'Edina talked to Miss Calder *before* we went and showed her the diamonds. So why did she pretend to be surprised?' She dropped her chin into her hands and sighed. 'I suppose she must have known they were there all along.'

Harry stood up. 'Right. No wonder she was mad at Miss Calder. She must have gone bananas when she found out she'd lent it to Dad.'

Charlotte sank her head onto her arms. 'This gets worse. I can't believe it. Edina is one of Dad's oldest friends. He's known her for ages. How can she be involved in something illegal?'

Harry began to pace around the table. 'No wonder she wanted to hang onto the reliquary,' he said. 'And no wonder she didn't want us to ring the police.' He slapped his hand on the table. 'Well, I'm going to ring them right now.' And he walked over to the phone on the worktop.

Charlotte leaped up and grabbed his arm before he could pick it up.

'Wait,' she said. 'Let's think about this. What if Dad's in it with her? He could be, couldn't he?'

Harry stood face to face with Charlotte. 'And what do you think, sis? Can you see Dad doing anything illegal? He won't even cheat at Monopoly. Whatever's going on, Dad's not a part of it and you know it.'

Charlotte slumped back onto the chair, twiddling her ponytail. 'You're right, Harry,' she said. 'But you still can't go to the police.'

'Why?'

'Because they'll never believe a couple of kids. Edina will deny everything we tell them. We've no evidence. She's got the reliquary and there's no evidence of the break-in. We cleared up, didn't we?'

'So?'

'I've told you before. If the police find out we're here on our own, the Social Services will take us into care.'

Harry knew it was all true and very depressing.

'We need that reliquary,' said Harry. 'That would be evidence.'

'Sure,' said Charlotte. 'And how are we going to get it back?'

Harry paced backwards and forwards. Somehow, he had to think of something.

8
Return to Edina

Darkness fell. Harry and Charlotte had grown used to the idea of being alone in the flat. Dad wouldn't come back that night, they felt certain. But they had decided that tomorrow they would go and fetch the reliquary. Then, if Dad was still missing, they would take it to the police.

All that evening they sat together in the living room, discussing how to retrieve the little box from Edina's house. Harry put forward one idea. Charlotte another and another. No matter what they came up with, nothing worked.

'It's impossible,' said Charlotte, throwing her hands in the air. 'None of our plans will get the reliquary back.'

'But *my* way is the *least* impossible,' said Harry, thrusting his chin forward, determined he was right. 'We might be in with a chance.'

Charlotte was having none of it. 'You might be in with a chance. But *I'm* not doing it.' She sank back on the sofa, turning her head away from her brother.

Harry stood up. His sister was too obstinate for

words. 'All right then, if *I* go back to Edina's house and *I* do a bit of tricksy acting – I know just what to say – then I reckon *I* could do it by myself.'

Charlotte snorted. 'No way. It's crazy. You know it is. No, no, no.'

Tired, worried and depressed, they went to bed, hoping their brains would come up with a better solution while they slept. Maybe there really was an easy answer to the problem.

But by the next morning, Harry's wild idea was still the only one with even an incy-wincy bit of hope of succeeding. Reluctantly, finally, Charlotte agreed.

'I don't approve of this stupid scheme,' she said as they sat eating bowls of Cheerios. 'I'll go with you, Harry, but I'm not in on the action. Right?'

'Right,' said Harry. 'Whatever.'

Shortly after eight o'clock, they put on their helmets and waterproof jackets and set off, riding in the early morning traffic through the Grassmarket. Rain was falling heavily and they had to take care not to skid. Twice they had to stop so that Harry could wipe his glasses and, by the time they had reached Dean Terrace, water was trickling off their helmets and running down the back of their necks.

Wet and miserable and irritated with her brother's mad plan, Charlotte climbed off her bike and pushed it along the pavement on the opposite side to the houses. This way she had some shelter from the overhanging trees. Once she reached a spot where she could clearly see Edina's house, she leaned her bike against the railings and stood with her arms folded, watching Harry put his plan into action. My brother is totally crazy, she thought. Why does he have to try out such a brainless idea? He is so annoying.

While Charlotte simmered, Harry hid between two parked cars, keeping watch on the black door with the lion's head knocker. He had seen several people come out of their houses and set off for work. But Edina's door stayed firmly shut. Then, just before half past nine, a small woman in a brown coat came down the street, walked up the steps to the black door and put her key in the lock. This, Harry knew, was Mrs McFee, Edina's housekeeper.

As the rain continued to fall, Harry shivered with the cold. Edina had not yet left the house and he wondered if Charlotte had been right after all. Maybe it was a mad idea. Maybe they should go back home. He glanced across at his sister standing sulking by the railings and was about to go and speak to her when the black door suddenly opened and Edina Ross stepped out. His pulse rate increased dramatically and went off the scale. His plan was now possible, he knew it!

9
A Little White Lie

Edina's car was parked a few metres from the front door. Harry knew it well. A silver Jaguar XJR with alloy wheels and chrome exhaust pipes. She opened the door with a click and climbed in. What a car, he thought, as she started the engine. Even the roar of the exhaust was impressive when she drove away.

Once she was out of sight, Harry stepped out from between the cars, onto the pavement. He turned and signalled a thumbs-up to Charlotte. With his heart beating dangerously fast, he climbed the steps and knocked on the door three times. It seemed like a million years before the door slowly opened and he saw Mrs McFee standing there. Her steely grey hair was drawn back from her lined face, and the black dress she wore was covered with a large flowery apron.

'Yes?' she said, scowling.

'Er . . . It's me, Mrs McFee. Harry Brodie. Remember?'

She leaned forward and screwed up her eyes to get a better look.

'I've come to see Edina.'

'She isn't in, I'm afraid,' she said. 'You'll have to come back another time.' And she began to close the door.

'I came yesterday and she helped me with some research for my school work,' he lied. 'Medieval period.'

'Well, she can't help you now,' Mrs McFee insisted. 'I told you, she's out.' She stepped back but Harry wouldn't let her go.

He placed his hand flat on the door and jammed his right foot against the hinge to prevent it from shutting. 'I left some books here. I expect they're in the sitting room. Sorry, but I need them today. It's really important.'

Mrs McFee sighed heavily, thinking of the effort it would take to climb those stairs. Harry saw her hesitate and took his chance.

'I can fetch the books,' he said, pushing past her. 'Edina won't mind, Mrs McFee.' He smiled at her. 'I'll find them and I'll let myself out. No need to bother you again. Will that be OK?'

She was about to protest when a timer pinged and the smell of cooking drifted down the hall. Harry guessed she was anxious to return to the kitchen.

'I suppose it'll be all right,' she muttered, turning to go back and check the oven. 'Don't be long, mind.'

As she shuffled away, Harry dashed up the stairs yelling, 'Thanks, Mrs McFee.'

There were twenty steps to the first landing. When Harry reached the top, he ran past the sitting room and two other doors before he came to the second flight of stairs. Edina had taken the reliquary up to her study, he remembered. It shouldn't be too hard to find it.

Up the stairs and onto the second landing, Harry flung open the first door he came to. No deal. It was Edina's bedroom. Of course, thought Harry, it was directly over the sitting room. And, just like the room below, it was full of antique furniture with heavy curtains at the window. This was definitely not a study. No time to stare. Hurry. Hurry. Hurry. He had to move on. He must find the reliquary and get out, pronto.

On to the next door. Open wide. Yes! It was Edina's study. No doubt about it. There was a computer on a large mahogany desk, two filing cabinets and a black leather chair. Bullseye! This was it. On the wall behind the desk, a wide shelf was crammed full of objects. Boxes made of gold and silver. Crosses. Small statues.

Then, right in the middle, Harry saw what he had been looking for.

The reliquary.

His mouth broke into a wide grin and he had to stop himself from shouting 'Yeah!' at the top of his voice. Instead, he balled his fist and silently punched the air, feeling very, very smug. He couldn't help wondering why Charlotte had made all that fuss. His plan had been a work of genius and he had pulled it off brilliantly. He couldn't wait to see the look on her face when he showed her the reliquary.

It was just as he reached over to take it off the shelf that the phone rang. The noise in the small study made him jump and started his pulse racing again. He stared as it rang six times, before the answerphone cut in and a man with a strong East European accent began to speak.

'Edina, I have changed my mind,' he said. 'You must bring our little box here immediately – with its contents, of course. Remember we have a new consignment arriving tonight. No more stupid slip-ups . . . You must be aware that I do not suffer fools gladly and I am seriously considering your future. Just one more mistake and I shall have to take steps.'

As Harry listened, his mouth fell open. His instinct

about Edina Ross had been right. She was involved in serious criminal activity. But what about Dad? What had happened to him? Was his disappearance linked to the reliquary?

Harry's heart pounded against his ribs as he grabbed the box – the valuable evidence they needed to show the police. They would investigate the crime and somehow – he wasn't sure how – but somehow, they could get Dad back.

Then, as he turned to go, the worst thing happened. Below in the hall, he heard the front door open and someone called out, 'Mrs McFee! I'm back.'

Edina Ross had returned.

10
Give-Away Trail

Harry opened the study door and listened.

'Mrs McFee!' Edina called as her footsteps clicked down the hall. The kitchen door opened. 'I forgot my mobile. Left it on the hall table.'

He heard her footsteps hurrying back towards the front door and he crossed his fingers. Please go, he prayed. Please go. Please go.

Then she stopped and he waited to hear her open the front door. He waited, chewing on his fingernails, his heart beating wildly. He waited. But the noise he heard next was not what he expected. From the bottom of the stairs, Edina gave a strange, strangulated cry. It was a cross between a gasp and a shout.

'Mrs McFee!' she called. 'Come here please.'

Harry heard the housekeeper's sloppy footsteps as she hurried from the kitchen.

'What are these muddy marks on the stairs?' Edina snapped. 'How did they get there?'

Suddenly Harry's heart stopped beating. He groaned inwardly and dropped his head onto his hand, covering his eyes. In his race to get upstairs, he had forgotten to take off his trainers and they had left a give-away trail of dirt. How far it had gone? he wondered. He looked down at the carpet in the study and then he peeped out at the landing. There were no foot-prints. He closed his eyes and blew out a lungful of air. Thank goodness. The first steps must have wiped the dirt off his trainers. Even so, those few marks could be enough to ruin his plan.

'It wasn't me,' Mrs McFee protested. 'I never go up in my outdoor shoes. Never.'

'Then who . . .?'

'It must have been that boy. That's who done it.'

'What boy?' Edina sounded angry.

'A laddie called round. Said he'd left a book here yesterday. I think his name was Harry.'

There was a pause then Edina said, 'Ah, Harry Brodie. Of course.' She sounded almost calm. Chilling, in fact.

'He was very polite,' the housekeeper insisted. 'Very considerate. He said he'd let himself out when he'd got the book.'

'Yes, yes, Mrs McFee. I understand,' Edina said. 'And did you see him leave?'

'No, but . . .'

'Then he's probably still looking for his . . . er . . . book,' she said. 'No problem. It's quite all right. I'll go and speak to him.'

As Edina walked up the stairs, she called, 'Harry, are you there, poppet?' and a cold shiver ran down Harry's spine. He looked round the small study for a place to hide. But there was nowhere. Whatever happened, he had to get out and find somewhere else. Edina mustn't find him. He had to keep the reliquary safe.

11
Dangerous Phone Call

Edina's bedroom was only a few metres away. Harry remembered a huge wardrobe which would make the perfect place to hide until she had left the house again. He scuttled along the corridor to the bedroom door and slipped inside. He had barely closed the door before he heard Edina call again.

'Are you still here, poppet? Mrs McFee told me you'd come.'

Harry panicked. She was already on the landing and very, very near. No time to dither. He flung himself flat and slid under the bed, holding his breath as he listened. She stopped for a moment outside the bedroom and Harry squeezed his eyes tight and counted, hoping she would go away. Then he heard the floorboards creak as she moved on to the study. Silence. She must be checking it out, he thought. She would notice that the reliquary had gone. He heard her slam the door shut and retrace her steps. Surely she would go back down to the hall now. She would think he had left and maybe she would leave, too.

For the moment he felt safe and he let out a huge sigh of relief.

But, just as Edina passed the door of the bedroom, the strident tones of Harry's mobile rang out from his pocket. 'Rudolph the Red Nosed Reindeer.' Full volume. Repeating. Getting louder and louder.

Because it was in the back pocket of Harry's jeans, it was almost impossible to reach it in the confined space under the bed. Somehow, he managed to wriggle to manoeuvre his arm behind his back, scraping his skin on the rough canvas underside of the bed as he did so. But finally he tugged the phone out of his pocket. It was still playing that crazy song as Harry pressed the OFF button and then he flung the mobile from under the bed, sending it into the corner of the room. Exhausted, he flopped back onto his stomach, face down and panting, as the door opened.

'Harry,' Edina called softly as she walked in. 'Is that you, sweetie? Where are you?'

Harry pushed his glasses up his nose as he peered from under the bed. He could see Edina's high-heeled shoes and the hem of her long, multi-coloured skirt as she stood in the doorway. She was looking round, trying to discover where the ringing had come from.

'Harry,' she said again as she stepped nearer to the

bed. Now she was so close that he could have reached out and touched her foot.

The shoes turned towards the window and stopped. 'Ah, there you are,' she said.

Harry held his breath, waiting to be dragged from his hiding place but instead he saw her hand reach down and pick his mobile off the carpet.

'So you've been in my bedroom, have you?' She was talking to herself now and her voice was less than friendly. 'Careless child. Losing your mobile, like that.' She raised her foot and brought the heel of her shoe crashing onto the phone, breaking it into several pieces.

From under the bed, Harry watched her kick the bits to one side before she marched out of the door and hurried down the stairs. The relief that swept over him was short-lived.

'Mrs McFee,' he heard Edina call. 'Come at once and help me look for that boy. He's here, somewhere. I'm sure of it.'

Harry's forehead broke out into a sweat. How long had he got before they found him? He had to get out of the house. Fast.

He wriggled out from under the bed and looked in the en-suite bathroom for an escape route. But there was only a small window with frosted glass. It would be difficult to get out through it and he wasn't sure what was on the other side. That left two options: walk out onto the landing and face Edina or climb out of the bedroom window.

As far as Harry was concerned, there was only one choice.

He hurried across to the tall sash window which faced the street. He flicked the catch that held it shut and pushed the bottom part of the window up half a metre or so. Then he ripped off his jacket and wrapped it round the reliquary. As he tossed the bundle out of the window, he prayed that Charlotte would see it fall and pick it up. At least if Edina walked in now, she wouldn't find the box.

Harry's brain was racing, plotting his getaway from the window. He knew that Dean Terrace had two types of houses. Edina Ross's house was four storeys high and butted up against a row of smaller houses which had two floors and an attic and – most importantly – there was a balustrade. If he shuffled along a narrow ledge which ran under the bedroom window, he could edge his way along and climb onto the balustrade of the next house. From there, he would be able to walk to the far end of the terrace, well away from Edina.

It wouldn't be easy. There was very little to hang on to before he reached the balustrade. The ledge was no more than four centimetres wide. If he wobbled, if he slipped, he would fall and crash onto the pavement below.

But there was no alternative. If he stayed here, he would be found. Edina would take the reliquary and, because of what he knew, his life would be in danger for sure.

No, there was no alternative. He would have to take a chance.

12
On the Edge

Harry heaved the window up higher to make more space and noticed that the curtains were tied back with cord looped over a hook on the wall. The cord could be useful. He pulled it from round one of the curtains, tugging it to test its strength. It was thick and strong and could take his weight if he slipped. He tied one end firmly to the hook and twisted the other end round his left wrist. He was ready to go.

He lifted one leg through the opening. He sat for a moment straddling the windowsill, feeling the power of the wind. He glanced down at the street below and felt his stomach shrink with fear as he gripped a tight hold of the cord and swung his other leg out so that both feet were on the ledge. Rain was still falling relentlessly and he knew the ledge would be slippery. He would have to be extra careful.

Nervously, he took his first small step to the right, tugging onto the cord. The ledge was so narrow that only the front half of his trainer fitted onto it. The rest was hanging out over the space beneath. He moved his left foot along to meet the other and, when his feet were close together, he let out a little more of the cord and pushed his right foot further along the ledge.

Harry didn't see the chip in the stone ledge. He didn't realize it was there until his trainers caught on it and suddenly he teetered, about to lose his balance. His head began to spin. But the cord held him and before he lost his footing completely, he grabbed hold of the window frame, yelling as he flopped over the sill.

He stayed in a heap on the floor, shaking uncontrollably, his heart pounding until he heard footsteps racing up the stairs. He scrambled to his feet. Again he began his escape, taking care to avoid the chip in the ledge – stepping faster this time, gripping onto the wall with one hand and the cord with the other. One step . . . two steps . . . three . . .

Then he heard what he dreaded most: the bedroom door had been flung open and someone was running towards the window. Harry was two metres from the balustrade. He shouldn't have glanced back – but he did. He saw Edina leaning through the window. She was reaching out to grab the cord to pull him off the ledge. Just one tug – that's all it would take.

He knew it was no good holding onto it. This was his last chance. He had to make the leap towards the balustrade. A good, strong leap. If he jumped short, he would plunge to the pavement and certain death.

He tried to steady himself.

And then he let go.

13
Catch Me If You Can

Charlotte had been waiting in the street for what seemed like hours. She was wet and cold and very irritated. Harry's plans were always crazy. Never as good as he thought and usually ending in some sort of trouble. She leaned on the railings and watched the comings and goings along the street. Edina Ross had left the house some time ago and driven away — presumably to the museum. Then Charlotte had seen Harry persuade Mrs McFee to let him in. Well, she thought, let's see if he finds the reliquary.

She was surprised when, not long after Harry had gone in, the silver Jaguar returned and Edina went back inside the house. This was going to be interesting. How was he going to get out of this one? she wondered. At least Edina had no idea that they suspected her of some kind of criminal activity. Harry would probably spin a brilliant yarn. She wished she could be a fly on the wall. She'd love to hear what he said.

When after quite a while her brother didn't come

out, her irritation grew. He was probably eating biscuits and drinking juice, she thought, while she stood and waited in the rain. It was time to act. She wanted to go home. She would ring his mobile and tell him to get a move on.

She pulled her mobile from the pocket of her jeans and hit Harry's number on her speed dial. She clamped it to her ear and listened as Harry's phone rang out. Then it went dead. Charlotte snapped her mobile shut, furious with her brother. She was certain he had *deliberately* switched it off because he didn't want to talk to her.

'If he thinks,' Charlotte said to herself, 'that I'm hanging round here in the miserable rain waiting for him, he's got another think coming. I'm off.'

She grabbed hold of her bike and swung her leg over ready to leave when something on the second floor caught her eye. The window opened and she saw someone lean out.

'Harry!' she called, dropping her bike and running across the road. But Harry didn't call back. He simply flung a parcel out of the window. As it fell, Charlotte stretched out her hands to catch it. But she was never much good on the sports field and she was useless at cricket, so she missed it by a few centimetres. Instead, it struck her forearm before bouncing onto the paving stones. The parcel was made up of Harry's coat and, when it fell open, she saw that the reliquary was inside.

Charlotte picked the bundle off the pavement and clutched it to her chest before running back across the road and stuffing it into her saddlebag. Why had Harry thrown it out of the window? She hadn't a clue.

When she turned again and glanced back at the window, she gasped to see Harry climbing out of the window and onto a narrow ledge. He clung on, gripping the stone face of the building like a climber on a sheer rock face. Had he gone completely crazy?

Charlotte watched, her heart pounding, her mouth open. And when Harry suddenly slipped, she let out a cry of horror. He was going to fall. But no. Harry had grabbed hold of the window frame and Charlotte breathed again – until, seconds later, he began another attempt. She couldn't watch. She clamped her hands over her face, too terrified to look, and when she pulled them away again, her brother had gone.

Harry was dead, she was certain of it. She darted across the road, expecting to see Harry lying lifeless on the pavement. But there was no sign of him. She looked over the railings into the basement to the side of the front steps. Nothing. Harry couldn't have fallen, after all. She glanced back up at the window on the second floor and she saw Edina's housekeeper sliding the window down, pulling it shut. So Harry must be inside. Someone had grabbed him and pulled him off the ledge.

At least he was alive.

Not knowing what to do next, Charlotte went back to her hiding place and stood shivering – whether with cold or wet or fear, she didn't know. Her only thought was that her brother was being held against his will. Now what should she do? Think, think, think. Her brain felt as if it had been stuffed into a liquidizer and turned into soup. She slumped against the railings and shut her eyes hoping that, when she opened them again, Harry would walk out of the door and wave to her and tell her he was OK.

That was what she hoped.

But it didn't happen.

She had been standing under the dripping trees for twenty minutes, half an hour – she wasn't sure – when a hot-dog van with a noisy exhaust came down Dean Terrace. Thick grey smoke was pouring out behind and it backfired twice before coming to a stop outside Edina Ross's house.

Charlotte recognized it at once. It was bright yellow

with a plastic hot dog on the roof. It was the van Harry had seen parked in the Grassmarket yesterday.

The man in the driver's seat reached through the open window to turn the handle. 'This is a right rubbish old banger,' he barked, flinging the door open. He climbed out, stretched his long legs and scratched the black stubble on his head. 'It's a bloomin' wonder we got here. Couldn't you find something better?' He slammed the door shut before feeling in his pocket for a cigarette.

Charlotte saw that his passenger was already standing on the pavement, a cigarette hanging from the corner of his mouth. In contrast to his mate, he was small with a thick neck and a large stomach. His hair, which was thin and curly, was red – not fiery red like Harry's – but a sort of ginger.

The small man smiled. 'Sure, it's not a bad old van, Kevin,' he said. 'Me brother did us a favour, lending it us.'

'Did he?' snapped the other. 'And if it breaks down and we can't do the job, Ivan Sikorsky'll kill us, I'm telling you.' Then he thumped his workmate in the shoulder, sending him off balance and staggering along the pavement. 'You're a fool, Dermot.'

The two men, Kevin Butterworth and Dermot

Boyle, stood drawing on their cigarettes before dropping them onto the pavement and grinding them under the soles of their trainers. Charlotte watched them climb the steps and knock on the black door with the lion's head knocker.

'Sure, Mr Sikorsky had no need to get into such a strop with us yesterday,' Boyle said as they waited. 'I couldn't help it if the box thingy wasn't in the flat. We got the Brodie man, didn't we?'

Charlotte straightened her back and strained to hear what they were saying. Had she heard right? Were they talking about Dad? She stepped out from under the tree and crouched between two parked cars. Nearer now, she might be able to hear more clearly.

''Course we got him,' Butterworth sneered through gritted teeth. 'But he couldn't take a punch, could he? What a wimp.'

'Ah well,' said Boyle, nodding his head and smiling. 'Sure, he'll be well enough to talk tomorrow. Mr Sikorsky will find out what he needs to know, eh? He'll know how to get the truth. No worries.'

With that, the door opened and the two men stepped into Edina Ross's house.

14
Hot-Dog Men

Harry had been so near to escaping. One jump. That's all it would have taken. He had stood on the ledge, battered by the wind and struck by rain as sharp as needles, taking a lungful of air. Ready for the great leap to safety. But he had suddenly felt his arms gripped by Edina's hands.

He had gasped and struggled to get away, not thinking of the drop to the pavement below. But she had hung onto him until she managed to pull him inside.

So Harry had failed. Now he lay panting on the bedroom carpet, with Edina Ross and Mrs McFee standing over him.

'Get a towel, Mrs McFee,' Edina said. 'Harry has made a terrible mess on the carpet.' She smiled a sinister smile. 'That was a silly thing to do, sweetie – jumping out of the window.'

Harry looked up at her. 'No? Really? I do it all the time. It's my hobby.'

Edina's face clouded over. She tightened her lips

and glowered at him. 'Why did you come here, Harry? You weren't looking for a book, were you?'

Mrs McFee returned with a towel. 'No, you weren't,' she said. 'You lied to me, didn't you? And you know what happens to boys who tell lies.'

Harry shook his head. 'Sorry, I don't,' he said, pulling himself into a sitting position. 'We haven't done that at school, yet. It must be on the Year 8 curriculum.'

Edina raised her hand as if to strike him but she controlled her temper and let her arm drop.

'Now, Harry,' she said in a voice that was calm and chilling at the same time. 'Explain. What exactly were you doing in my house?'

He tried to think of a good explanation. But he couldn't. Nobody drops in uninvited then makes a death-defying exit from a second-floor window – not unless they've got something to hide.

When he didn't answer, Edina leaned forward. She was so close that her perfume made him feel sick and he tried to shuffle away from her but he felt the bed pressing into his back.

'You took the reliquary, didn't you?' she said so quietly that he had to strain to hear.

He gritted his teeth, determined not to answer.

'So where did you put it, Harry?' she said, leaning even closer. 'Tell me.'

Then Harry's temper snapped. 'It's not your property. It belongs to the museum,' he yelled. 'But I bet they don't know anything about the diamonds, do they?'

She straightened her back and smiled a dry, withering smile. 'Really, Harry. What do you know about museum business? You wouldn't understand.'

Harry wasn't having any of her patronizing you're-just-a-kid talk. He knew better than that.

'All the time you pretended to be our friend,' he said, 'but you're a crook, you are. I know—'

WHACK! Her hand landed a stinging blow across his cheek making him gasp. He stared back at her. Dad's friend had suddenly turned into Witch Woman.

She stepped back, clasping her hands behind her back. 'And what about your sister? Why didn't Charlotte come with you? Isn't she in on this?'

'No,' Harry lied. 'She's gone to our auntie's. I didn't tell her I was coming here. I wish I hadn't come myself now.'

'So do I,' Edina said, walking towards the door. 'I'm going to make a phone call now.' Then she glanced over her shoulder and said, 'Don't try anything, Harry.

Mrs McFee is not a dithering old lady. She is quite capable of keeping you under control.'

With that, she marched out of the room, her perfume hovering behind her in a sickly cloud. Harry was left sitting on the carpet, watched by Mrs McFee who now looked almost as scary as Edina Ross. Once she had wiped the carpet with the towel, she stood in front of him, arms folded, clutching a knobbly old walking stick in her right hand.

Harry sank his head onto his knees wondering how he was going to get out of this mess. He could hear Edina in her office, talking on the phone but she was too far away for him to hear what she said. What was going on? What were they going to do to him?

When she returned, she was smiling in a mean, smirking kind of way. 'You're a lucky boy, Harry. You're going on a trip.'

'With you?' he said. 'I think I'll give it a miss.' Going anywhere with Edina Ross was now at the bottom of his Things-to-Do wish list. 'But you could let me go home,' he added. 'I won't say a word. Promise.'

She wasn't even listening.

Time dragged and it seemed like hours passed before he heard a knock on the front door.

'Ah, that will be your chauffeur,' she said with a

silly little giggle. She walked out of the room and went downstairs. Harry heard her open the door and let somebody in.

When she walked back into the room, she was followed by Boyle and Butterworth and their over-powering stink of stale cigarettes, beer and sweat.

Under strict instructions from Edina, they had left their trainers in the hall. Unfortunately, this meant that their filthy socks were revealed with their grubby toes bursting through the holes like overcooked sausages.

'This him?' Butterworth asked, nodding at Harry.

'Obviously,' Edina replied. 'Mr Sikorsky wants to see him as soon as possible.'

Butterworth bent over to look more closely at Harry. 'A bit on the skinny side, isn't he?' Then he laughed.

Edina Ross pushed her hair back from her face. 'I presume the two of you can manage to take him?'

'No worries, lady,' Boyle said, flexing his biceps. 'We've got muscles like grapefruits. Sure you've never seen nothin' like 'em.'

'I don't wish to know about your muscles,' she sniffed. 'I want to make sure that the boy doesn't get away.'

Butterworth guffawed. 'Do we look as if we can't handle a kid?'

'No,' Boyle butted in. 'And we wouldn't want a good-looking lady like yourself messing up her nice clothes, now, would we?'

Edina Ross flushed with anger. 'I had no intention of doing so,' she said. 'And watch your personal remarks.'

Butterworth dug Boyle in the belly. 'Zip it! Show some respect and get a move on.'

The blow to Boyle's stomach had hurt his pride more than his body and Harry couldn't help but grin at the sight of him blushing with embarrassment.

'Something funny, eh?' Boyle said, thrusting his chin forward. He grabbed hold of Harry's arm, dragged him to his feet and shoved him towards the door.

Edina held up her hand. 'No,' she snapped. 'Hasn't it occurred to your tiny brains that he could escape as soon as you open the front door?'

Boyle looked bewildered.

'The boy will be off like a guided missile,' she sneered. 'He can probably run twice as fast as you two overblown hedgehogs. Tie him up, for heaven's sake. Use your common sense.' And she left the room to go downstairs, followed by Mrs McFee.

Butterworth turned to Boyle. 'See! Use your common sense,' he said and biffed him again – this time on the shoulder. 'Go on. Tie him up, you great maggot.'

Even though Harry pressed his lips together, he couldn't stop a snigger bursting out and Boyle heard. 'You won't be laughing long,' he said and he went to pick up the cord that Harry had used in his escape attempt. He then took great pleasure in winding it tightly round Harry's chest, pinning his arms to his side.

It hurt. Harry yelled 'Aaaggghhh,' which seemed to please Boyle and he tugged the rope tighter. Butterworth fetched a cord from the other curtain and Boyle wound this one round Harry's legs so that he was trussed up like an oven-ready chicken.

'That's fixed yer, eh?' Boyle sneered. 'Get walkin', lad.' And Harry felt a terrible punch in the middle of his back. He tried to keep upright but it was impossible. First he wobbled and then, because he was unable to move his legs, he fell flat on his face.

'You great clown!' Butterworth snapped at Boyle. 'How can he walk with his legs tied together?'

Boyle glowered at Harry whom he blamed for all his trouble.

'Get him up,' yelled Butterworth. 'We'll carry him to the van. It'll be quicker.'

'Right you are,' said Boyle and put his hands under Harry's armpits while Butterworth lifted his knees.

But Harry wasn't going to go easily. He was determined to make it difficult for them. He twisted and turned. He wriggled and pushed. They couldn't keep hold of him. So when they had struggled through the bedroom door and were at the top of the stairs, Boyle let Harry slip.

'Fool! Idiot,' called Butterworth as Harry slithered out of their hands.

He felt himself falling, crashing on the stairs. Every vertebrae in his spine scraped on a sharp corner of the steps, bump, bump, bump, rubbing his back raw. Ow! Stop! It was agony.

He landed in a heap on the tiles in the hall near to where Edina Ross was waiting impatiently by the front door.

She sighed. 'Oh, for heaven's sake! Come and pick him up,' she said, flapping her hand towards Harry. 'Can't you two do anything properly?'

Boyle and Butterworth hurried down the stairs, jostling for lead position. 'It's all under control, ma'am,' said Butterworth. 'Leave it to me.'

But Edina was not convinced.

'I shall follow you in my car,' she said, reaching for

her keys. 'I have matters to discuss with Mr Sikorsky. I want to know what he plans to do about the boy and his father.'

With that, she opened the front door. Boyle and Butterworth picked Harry up like a sack of potatoes and carried him out of the house.

15
A Risky Journey

Charlotte had been waiting ever since the two men arrived. She had long since stopped worrying about her hair and her wet trainers. But she couldn't stop worrying about Harry and wondering what was going on inside the house. She glanced at her watch again. She had never known time go so slowly. And then, at last, the front door opened and the same two men stepped out, carrying a large bundle. When Charlotte realized that the bundle was Harry bound up like a Christmas parcel, her heart raced, banging against her ribs. She was terrified. Horrified. What were they doing to her brother? Where were they taking him?

She watched Boyle and Butterworth carry him to the yellow hot-dog van parked in front of Edina's Jaguar. She watched them open the doors at the back and stuff him inside, and she almost fainted with shock. They dumped him on the floor of the van as if he were no more than a sack of carrots. How could they!

Shaking with anger, she saw them slam the doors shut, walk round to the front and climb in. She had to stop them somehow. Quick. Before they pulled away. She could do it if she opened the doors and dragged Harry out of the van.

She stepped into the road, checking that Dean Terrace was deserted. Boyle was sitting in the passenger seat, talking to Butterworth. He wouldn't see her. Good. She was about to run across to the van, when Edina Ross came out of the house and Charlotte had to retreat behind a parked car.

'Did you lock the van doors?' Edina called to the men.

Butterworth, who was settled in the driver's seat, leaned out of the window. 'No. I didn't think—'

'Then do it, at once!' Edina yelled. 'We don't want him getting out, do we?'

'Absolutely not, ma'am. No, we certainly don't,' he called, leaping out of the van. 'It just slipped my mind. Good thing you mentioned it, ma'am. Good thinking.' He hurried round to the back and turned the key in the lock.

Silently Charlotte cursed her bad luck as Edina Ross walked towards the Jaguar and got in, ready to leave. What could she do now? There was no way she could find out where they were taking Harry. How could she help him?

As the van started up and lurched away from the kerb, its exhaust made an explosive noise. Charlotte's heart sank. Now the Jaguar would follow and she would be left behind.

But, as luck would have it, that didn't happen. Instead, Charlotte saw the car door open and Edina climb back out. She ran up the front steps, unlocked the door and went back into the house.

She's forgotten something, Charlotte thought. This is my chance. GO! GO! GO!

Keeping low, with her knees bent, she ran out from behind the parked car, crossed the street and crouched by the Jaguar, praying that no one would see. She opened the back door and slid inside, shutting it behind her. She spread herself full length on the floor, face down behind the front seats, waiting for Edina to return. If all went well, she would hitch a ride without being spotted. But if Edina should see her there . . .

She didn't dare think about it.

Charlotte lay on the floor of the car trying to slow down her breathing, waiting for the moment when Edina returned. She had never done anything this crazy or this dangerous before and she had no idea where it would lead. It was an impulse. Her one slim chance to save Harry.

It seemed only seconds after she had hidden in the back of the car that she heard the door open. Then Edina Ross slipped into the driver's seat, started up the engine and swung the Jaguar away from the kerb.

They were on their way.

Three minutes . . . four . . . five . . . Then Edina shouted, 'No! I don't believe it!' and Charlotte's pulse shot up to danger level. She felt the driver stamp on the brakes and the Jaguar swung hard to the left, sending her sliding along the small space and flinging her against the door. She wanted to yell, 'What are you doing?' but she stopped herself.

As it turned out, Edina's outburst was because she had glanced down at the petrol gauge – EMPTY – and she had pulled into a service station to fill up. Charlotte realized that there was a chance Edina might see her while she was filling the tank. She could easily glance inside the car and see her lying there. Then all would be over. She lay with eyes squeezed tight, hardly daring to breathe. 'Please, please, pleeeeeeeeeease,' she said to herself, over and over.

Luckily, Edina did not take her eye from the petrol gauge, frowning as the litres and pounds spun round. She tapped her foot, irritated that time was passing and she was well behind those stupid men, Boyle and Butterworth.

When the Jaguar set off again, the tyres vibrated on the bumpy cobbled roads of Edinburgh. This made for such an uncomfortable ride that Charlotte began to feel sick. Fresh air – that's what she needed, but she dared not lift her head as much as a centimetre in case she was spotted. So she stayed still with her nose touching the hairy carpet, breathing specks of fluff into her mouth and nostrils.

As the journey continued, a tickle grew in her throat until she was desperate to cough. It was torture. But which was worse – wanting to be sick or needing to cough? At that moment, her lungs were ahead in the Torture Stakes and they felt as if they were about to explode. Charlotte clapped her hand over her face, in a frantic attempt not to cough. When this wasn't enough to hold it, she stuffed the sleeve of her sweater into her mouth but she knew it was only a matter of minutes before her cough escaped and the driver would discover that she had an unwanted passenger.

Two things happened next.

Edina switched on the radio and, just for a second or two, she opened the window to let in a blast of air that carried with it the thunder of passing lorries.

These deafening noises gave Charlotte a brief opportunity to cough. Even so, she was careful, pulling her sweater over her head to muffle the sound.

It worked.

Charlotte relaxed, glad to be able to breathe freely again. Not only that, she no longer felt sick. The road was smoother now and there was very little jolting. She guessed that they were on a motorway or a main road at least. They had left Edinburgh behind.

16
Inside the Van

If Charlotte thought *her* journey was uncomfortable, it was nothing compared with Harry's. The back of the hot-dog van was mostly taken up by metal cupboards on one side and a fridge and cooker on the other. This was bad enough but there was a ladder taking up most of the space in between.

As the van bumped along, Harry was buffeted around on the floor. With every bend, he was flung from one side to the other. Even when he managed to wedge himself into a corner, the ladder slid around and crashed into his legs, again and again. At first, he tried yelling, 'Stop! Let me out of here!' but it was pointless. Nobody took any notice. Why would they?

Harry guessed they had been on the way for almost an hour when the van pulled off the road and began to roll over a rough, bumpy track, which was much worse. He could feel every bruise in his body. In fact, he felt as if he had turned into one giant bruise. There seemed to be nothing between his bones and the hard metal floor.

The bumping lasted for some time until the van came to a halt and the engine stopped. Harry slumped with relief, inhaled deeply and then puffed the air out through his lips. The journey was over. He couldn't think about anything else. Not 'What happens now?' or 'Where am I?' All he could cope with was the knowledge that the pain had stopped.

Outside, someone was opening a gate and people were talking. The engine started up again and the van moved forward slowly. Then it stopped once more and Harry heard the men climb out and slam the doors shut.

'What'll we do with the lad?' asked Boyle. 'Shall we drag him out? I'd like to show him a thing or two. See how polite he'll be then. Show me some respect, eh?'

Butterworth was already walking away. 'No. We'll go see the boss first.'

'Shall we leave him then, Kevin? Leave him, eh? Is that what you think?'

Butterworth sighed. 'He's not going anywhere, is he?'

Harry heard their footsteps and their banter fading as they walked from the hot-dog van. He wondered if he should feel relieved that they had gone or alarmed that he had been abandoned in a metal box on wheels.

Tough call.

17
Arrival

Boyle and Butterworth walked towards a crumbling stone building. It had once been a fine monastery but now it hunched, decayed and decrepit. The nearest village was miles away.

The two men paused outside the door, huddling in the alcove of a half-collapsed arch.

Butterworth knocked and waited.

'What are we going to tell him?' hissed Boyle, chewing on his fingernail.

'What are *you* going to tell him?' said Butterworth. 'I'm keeping my mouth shut. I've seen what happens to people who don't. The guy's a psycho. He's ex-KGB. Or didn't you know that?'

'That explains a lot. I saw the way he bullied these monks. I'm almost sorry for the poor idiots.'

'Don't be,' Butterworth snorted. He leaned on the wall and looked out at the fields where the monks were tending the garden. 'They're fools. They mess around with their pigs and their horses instead of getting out of here. What's to stop them escaping, huh?'

'Sure,' Boyle laughed, 'they're scared to death. That Father Abbot's locked up and the boss will kill the old fella if they put a foot wrong.'

At last they heard footsteps approaching down the hall. Then a tiny window in the door opened and an eye pressed against it before heavy bolts were drawn back and the door was opened.

A man dressed in a monk's habit stood in front of them. He was huge, like an ageing rugby player with a nose squashed flat and crooked. His hair was short as if it had been cut by a lawn mower and across his knuckles were tattooed the words LOVE and HATE.

'We've come to see the boss,' said Butterworth.

'You took your time. Where's the boy?'

'He's in the van.'

LOVE HATE leaned forward, glowering at Butterworth. 'He's no good there, is he? You'd better go and get him pronto!'

'Oh, yeah. Right. Will do,' said Butterworth. Then he turned to Boyle and thumped him on the shoulder. 'Don't stand there gawping. Go and get him.'

Boyle clutched his shoulder. 'Why me?' he whined.

''Cos I say so.'

'But how am I going to carry him? He's a big lad. I'm not sure I—'

'Oh, you're a weakling now, are you?' Butterworth sneered. 'Typical. If I want anything doing, I have to do it myself.' And he stomped away towards the van with Boyle skittering after him, muttering complaints and rubbing his bruises.

18
Inside the Monastery

While the men were away, Harry struggled to untie the rope. He rolled and twisted and kicked. But the knots were too high up his back to reach and he finally collapsed exhausted and furious, so that when he heard the key in the lock and the doors finally opened, his anger spilled out.

'About time,' he yelled. 'What do you think you're doing bringing me here? You're in dead trouble, you are!'

'Less of your lip,' Butterworth shouted back. 'We're taking you inside.'

'I'm not going anywhere!'

Butterworth turned to Boyle and nodded towards Harry. 'Go on. Get him out. They're waiting for him.'

But when Boyle leaned into the van and tried to grab hold of his legs, Harry kicked at him, catching him on the chin and sending him staggering backwards. Boyle's arms flailed in the air until finally he crashed onto the muddy ground.

'Oh, me chin!' he yelled. 'Oooooh, me leg!'

Seeing that the boy wasn't going to go quietly, Butterworth flung himself into the van. Harry felt his ribs crunch. The big guy was on top of him. 'Get off me,' he wheezed, but all that came out was a feeble kind of gasp, as if all the breath had been knocked out of him.

'I'll show you who's boss,' Butterworth snarled.

Then Boyle, who was already back on his feet and wiping his muddy hands on his jeans, shouted, 'I'm comin',' and joined in the battle.

Harry made life as difficult as possible for the two men. He wriggled and kicked as they pulled him from the van. He dug his teeth into Boyle's hand. He even shouted, 'Let me go! Help!' hoping someone would hear. He would not give up and when Butterworth and Boyle were really fed up with the struggle, they dumped him on the ground.

'Think you're clever, do yer?' said Butterworth standing over him. 'Right then, you can walk – or else we'll drag you through the mud.'

He bent down and untied the cord and Harry felt his legs released and his circulation flow down to his toes.

'That's a good idea,' Boyle said. 'Make him walk.

That'll show him.' Then Boyle pulled the cord from round Harry's chest and flung it into the van.

'NO!' Butterworth yelled. 'Idiot! I only wanted his *legs* free, you great booby.'

Boyle looked sheepish. 'Oh well. 'Tis done.'

'So what now?' said Butterworth, red in the face with anger. 'We let him run away, do we?'

Boyle spread his arms wide and looked into the distance. 'Ah sure – where's he going?' he said. And he was right. There was nothing but miles of heath land. There was nowhere to run.

'The point is,' snapped Butterworth, 'you didn't do what you were told, did you? You never do, do you? You've got a brain like a sieve.'

The men were on either side of Harry, Butterworth gripping his collar and Boyle pushing him forward with his fist. And when they reached the main entrance of the monastery, the man in the monk's habit with the LOVE HATE tattoos was waiting.

'Right,' said LOVE HATE. 'Bring him in quick. The boss is not in a good mood.'

Harry felt like a piece of baggage as they dragged him through the door, into the cloisters and along corridors – endless corridors. He had never seen such a rabbit warren of a place. He wondered how he would ever find his way out.

Finally, they stopped outside a large wooden door and LOVE HATE knocked.

Someone replied, 'Come,' and LOVE HATE opened the door and put his head round. 'The boy's here. Do you want me to send him in?'

'Send him in! Send him in! Have I not been waiting?'

The voice had a strong foreign accent. Eastern European, Harry thought. Not exactly friendly.

Boyle's fist sent Harry stumbling into the room so that he came face to face with a middle-aged man sitting behind a huge oak desk. He was small with powerful shoulders and smooth black hair spread across a potato-shaped head.

This was Harry's first meeting with Ivan Ivanovich Sikorsky.

The man leaned forward, his excessive belly squashing against the desk. He clasped his hands in front of him and rested them on the desk. For some time, he didn't speak but his dark eyes were fixed on Harry and seemed to bore into his brain like a black laser beam. There was no doubt about it, Harry thought, this was a powerful man. Controlling. Used to making people jump to his command. A bully.

Sikorsky pressed his fingers to his lips as if he was thinking, and still said nothing.

In the silence, Harry felt his heart thumping faster than it ever had. Faster and faster. Why was he just sitting there? he thought. Why didn't he say something? The waiting was agony. He couldn't stand it. Harry's forehead was soon damp with sweat, his hands trembled and his knees were slowly turning to jelly. He had never been more frightened in his life.

19
Tough Questions

Ivan Sikorsky dropped his hands to rest on the arms of the chair.

'So,' he said, 'you are the boy who broke into Miss Ross's house, no?' He leaned forward. 'It was you stole the reliquary. Is that so?'

Harry's mouth was dry as stale bread. 'It's none of your business,' was what he intended to say but when he tried to speak, he could only make small squawking noises.

'ANSWER ME!' Sikorsky yelled. 'You are a thief, no?'

Harry's voice finally came in a whisper. 'I didn't steal it.'

'What did you say? Speak up!' Sikorsky snapped, and spittle flew out of his lips and ran down his chin.

While he wiped it away with the back of his hand, Harry's fear was suddenly replaced with anger. Who was this nasty little man? What right had he to ask him questions?

'I didn't steal it,' Harry said, loud and clear. 'It wasn't

Edina's in the first place. And you've no right to bring me here. Don't you know it's against the law?'

Sikorsky snorted at his words. He narrowed his eyes and leaned back in his chair, staring at the boy in front of him. Then, slowly, he stood up and as he walked round the desk and came closer, Harry saw a scar running from his mouth up to his left eye. That must have been some fight. He wondered what had happened to the other man. Maybe Sikorsky had killed him. He couldn't imagine this man losing to anyone.

When Sikorsky was half a metre away, he stood still, staring at Harry. He began to speak slowly in a deep voice that was so calm it was frightening.

'Where is the reliquary? Tell me.'

By now, Harry's legs were trembling so badly that he found it hard to stand. 'I . . . I don't know where it is.'

'You are sure?' the man snarled.

'Yes. And if I knew I wouldn't tell you.'

In the deathly silence that followed, Sikorsky reached out and grasped Harry's wrists. 'Are you *really* sure, boy?'

'I . . . I don't know where it is, honest.'

Then Harry felt the pain. His wrists were squeezed in a grip so strong he was sure his bones would snap.

Nobody could have fingers this powerful. His mouth fell open gasping for air. Stop! he wanted to cry out. He wanted to scream. But he couldn't.

Then relief came as Sikorsky released his grip. 'I do not believe you,' he said. Now his nose was almost touching Harry's and he could smell his breath. 'I repeat: where is the reliquary?' The Russian paused between each word.

'I don't know,' Harry said and Sikorsky took hold of his wrists again.

Even before he felt the pain, Harry let out a cry and shrank from him, unable to bear the thought of more punishment. He turned his head away not daring to look at his attacker. 'I threw it out of the window,' he said.

Sikorsky smiled. He grasped Harry's chin and forced him to look directly into his eyes. 'Is that true, my friend? Because if it isn't . . .'

'Yes, yes. It's true. I threw it out. I threw it into the street.'

Colour rose in Sikorsky's face as he turned on Boyle and Butterworth. 'Did you two fools think to look in the street, eh?' He stepped towards them and prodded each in the chest with a steely finger. 'Do you ever use the brains, you stupid, stupid men?'

Butterworth and Boyle cowered like frightened pups.

'W . . . we went to pick up the boy,' said Butterworth, shifting nervously from one foot to the other. 'We didn't know nothin' about finding no reliquary.'

In exasperation Sikorsky waved his arms in the air, flapping the two men away like pesky flies.

'Go! Go! You annoy me, you fools. Go back to Dean Terrace and don't come back without the reliquary or . . .' He didn't need to finish the sentence. They knew what would happen.

Boyle and Butterworth had become gibbering idiots. They nodded nervously and turned to go – but not without bumping into each other as they tried to leave.

'WAIT!' Sikorsky shouted. 'Do not leave the boy here. Lock him up. NOW! I decide what to do with him later.'

They jumped at his order. They grabbed Harry and dragged him through the door. But, as they pulled him into the corridor and were about to take him away, Sikorsky called again. 'One moment!'

The men responded at once, turning round and dashing back into the room. That was their mistake.

Boyle thought Butterworth was holding Harry.

Butterworth thought Boyle was holding Harry.

In that split second, Harry broke away. He ran as he had never run before. Down the corridor, in the direction they had come.

'You let him go, you great lummuck!' Butterworth yelled at Boyle and whacked him across the head.

'Aaaagghhh,' screamed Boyle.

'Run after him!' yelled Butterworth.

While Butterworth and Boyle were arguing and Sikorsky was shouting, Harry was well ahead of them. Even when the two men had set off running, they were slow and lumbering so Harry had a chance to get out of the building before they caught up with him. Which way to go? If only he could find his way through the maze of passages.

He ran and when he saw a metal trolley standing against the wall, he leaped onto it, pushing with one foot like a scooter, scattering its load of boxes as he went. The wheels zipped over the stone floor at a terrific speed so that his lead over Boyle and Butterworth was increasing every second. Ahead of him was a door that led to the cloisters. He was nearly there. At last, Harry gave a final push for freedom.

20
No *En Suite*

BANG!

When he smashed into the door, he expected it to swing open. He expected to burst through.

But he didn't.

The door stayed firmly shut. Of course it did. It opened inwards. So Harry was flung back, landing with a crunch on the hard floor, knocking his glasses off his nose and the breath out of his lungs. He cursed his own stupidity as he reached out and patted his hands across the floor, hoping to feel his glasses. No time. Footsteps sounded down the corridor. They were coming for him. They were near. Harry got to his feet and grasped the door handle. He turned the knob and pulled the door open. Hallelujah! He was on his way again.

But no. His way was blocked. Something big. A great black mountain. He squeezed his eyes to help him see better and there in front of him was a large monk. Harry looked up and recognized the face of LOVE HATE, who immediately reached forward and grabbed Harry with his huge meaty hands.

'You're not going anywhere, son,' he said. 'You're coming with me.' He took Harry by the collar and dragged him back down the corridor.

Boyle and Butterworth were limping towards them, gasping for breath. The chase had been too much for them.

When they reached Sikorsky's office, he was standing by the door, his hands on his hips with his mouth fixed in an expression of disgust.

'How many times do I say it, huh?' he said. 'You two are stupid? No?'

'No,' squeaked Boyle. 'Er . . . I mean yes.'

LOVE HATE smirked and passed Harry over to Butterworth and Boyle.

'Take the boy down to the cellar,' screamed Sikorsky. 'You can do that simple thing, yes?'

They nodded like frightened five-year-olds.

Once again that afternoon, Harry had got the better of Boyle and Butterworth but now they would get their own back. They gripped Harry's bruised arms so tightly that he yelped with pain as they walked him down the corridor.

'Now then,' Butterworth said as they stopped outside a small door, 'see how you like this.' And he pushed him through. 'This good enough for yer?'

he said as he clicked the light switch and Harry saw a set of stone steps in front of him disappearing into darkness.

'Go on,' said Boyle. 'Sure, you can walk down steps, can't you? Or do you need a push?'

Harry could feel the temperature dropping as he walked down.

'Would you mind turning the central heating on?' he said.

Butterworth prodded him. 'You'll enjoy the cold, son,' he said. 'This is where the old monks kept their food. They put their butter and meat on those slabs over there. Not many people know that.'

'Why would they do that?' asked Boyle. 'Didn't they have fridges or nothin'?'

'Where's your education?' Butterworth snapped. 'In those days they didn't have no electricity never mind refrigerators.'

At the bottom of the steps was a wide passageway with a vaulted brick ceiling, lit by a single light bulb. But Harry was overwhelmed by the sickening smell of bad drains or something rotting.

'I think a couple of rats died in here,' said Harry. 'Is Mr Sikorsky missing any of his men?'

Butterworth ignored him. He went to open a tall

cupboard at the far end. There was a small grille in the door and the cupboard had probably been used for storing food. A kind of pantry, Harry thought.

'Sorry there's not enough room for a bed,' sneered Butterworth, 'but it's the best we can do.'

'Haven't you got anything with an *en suite?*' Harry mocked as he looked at the cramped space. 'I feel like a bath before I go to sleep.'

Boyle stepped forward to push him inside but Harry was too quick for him. He turned and lashed out with a tae-kwon-do kick, strong and vicious. Crack! It made contact with Boyle's kneecap and he doubled up in pain.

'Oh, me knee!' he yelled as Harry twisted and kicked again. But this time, Butterworth grabbed his leg.

'Don't try to be smart, kid,' he said and Harry felt himself propelled backwards into the cupboard and heard the door slam shut.

Boyle was groaning and rubbing his knee.

'Get the key, Dermot,' Butterworth said. 'We have to make sure he doesn't get away.'

'Can't you get it?'

'No. I'm in charge. You get it.'

Boyle limped over to the far wall, muttering complaints as he went. He took a key off a hook and limped back.

'That'll sort him out,' he said as he handed the key to Butterworth.

Harry slumped onto the stone floor as he heard the key turn in the lock. He felt angry with himself. Why hadn't he put up a better fight? Why hadn't he bitten them, scratched them, head-butted them?

But the truth was Harry was bruised like a rotten apple. He hurt all over and he was exhausted. He wanted to sleep – preferably in his own bed.

But there was no bed. Only a stinking tin bucket in the corner, a disgusting substitute for a toilet.

Boyle and Butterworth's footsteps were fading into the distance. They were already halfway up the steps. But if Harry thought things couldn't get worse, he was wrong. Before the two men opened the door at the top of the stairs, Boyle flicked the light switch, cutting out the light that had filtered through the small grille. The cellar was plunged into a darkness as thick as treacle.

Harry's spirits sank into a pit of despair. He curled into a ball and wondered if he would ever get out.

21
Up the Chimney

The silver Jaguar slowed down and stopped. The engine died and Charlotte heard Edina Ross snap off her seat belt, open the door and slam it shut behind her.

She lay still, listening to Edina's footsteps on the gravel getting fainter. And, when she couldn't hear them at all, she pulled herself up until her eyes were level with the window and peered out. Yes! The Jaguar was parked right next to that stupid hot-dog van. It was just as she had hoped. Harry was here.

But there were a million questions she needed to answer. For a start – *why* were they here? It was just a crumbling old building. Nothing else.

She turned and peered out of the back window. On the far side of a field, monks in black habits were working in a vegetable garden. There were pigs, too. Fat pink pigs with black spots and one, bigger than the rest, had the biggest tusks she had ever seen. Weird. And in another field there were two shaggy horses grazing. So why would Edina Ross and those two thugs come to a monastery? Charlotte wondered. It was a mystery.

When she was sure no one was near enough to see her, she reached out for the handle to open the door. But when she pulled the handle, nothing happened. She tried again, harder this time but it still wouldn't open. Had she been locked inside? Was she trapped? Then it occurred to her that the back doors were fitted with child locks and couldn't be opened from the inside. The only way to get out was to climb into the front seat and use the driver's door.

She squeezed through the small space between the two front seats. And when her sweater caught on the gear lever, she cursed 'Oh knickers!' She was stuck. She twisted and turned, trying to pull the sweater free, and when it was, she dragged her feet through the gap and into the front.

'Phew!' she said as she finally climbed out of the car. Then she ran over to the van to see if Harry was still inside. She peeped through the sliding window where they served the hot dogs but she couldn't see much. Instead, she tapped on the side and called, 'Harry, are you in there?' several times and pressed her ear against the door. In a last attempt, she went round to the back and found that the doors had been left unlocked.

'Bingo!' she said and flung the doors open. No Harry. So they must have taken him into the building, she thought.

She raced across the car park and stepped into the porch. The main door of the monastery was slightly ajar as if the last person to go through hadn't bothered to shut it properly. She slipped inside and found herself in an empty hallway with an oak staircase tucked into one corner and a gloomy corridor stretching ahead. Before she had made up her mind which way to go, she heard a door click open and she darted into the space under the staircase, afraid of being seen. A monk emerged from a side room. Should she talk to him? Should she tell him that her brother had been brought here? But could she trust him? Even a holy man – how could she be sure? She decided against it and flattened herself against the wall, hoping he wouldn't come her way. She listened to his feet on the stone floor and, when she heard the bang of another door closing, she peeped out to find the corridor empty again.

The building was old and complex. If she had any hope of finding Harry, she knew she would have to search it room by room. She stepped out of her hiding place and walked softly down the corridor until she came to an oak door. Only the creak of the hinges

100

disturbed the quiet of the old building and she found herself standing in a deserted dining room. It was empty except for a long refectory table and twelve chairs. But Charlotte noticed another door at the far end of the room. Was Harry behind it? she wondered. She hurried past the table, fixing her eye on the door. But suddenly angry voices erupted from the other side of that door and footsteps were coming her way.

Charlotte felt panic rise in her throat. There was no time to run back the way she had come. Frantically looking around for somewhere to hide, she saw nothing. If she hid under the table she would easily be spotted. She turned and stared at a large open fireplace and knew it was her only chance. She looked up the chimney. Was it wide enough to take her? If she got a foothold, maybe she could hide up there until they had gone.

The door at the far end opened.

Charlotte, already in the fireplace, reached up and grabbed hold of the soot-covered bricks and pulled her legs up behind her. She wedged herself firmly, her back pressing against one side and her feet pressing against the other. She had hardly fixed her position when two people walked into the dining room.

22
Conversation Overheard

'This is a disaster!' Those were the first words Charlotte heard as the two people walked into the dining room. They were spoken by a man – foreign, she guessed, and very angry. 'When your friend Brodie wakes, we question him. He is nothing to you, huh?'

'Nothing,' a woman replied. 'Nothing at all.'

Charlotte recognized the voice of Edina Ross and, gasping at what she heard, she let her hands slip. Quickly, she recovered and braced herself again in the chimney, her fingers gripping the rough cutting surface of the brick. The footsteps came nearer as they walked through the dining room. And when the couple reached the fireplace, they stopped. Charlotte clung on, more frightened than ever. They were horribly near. If they looked up, they might see her, or hear her breathing, or hear her heart thumping. She was terrified. The muscles in her arms and legs screamed out with the strain of keeping herself safe. Could she hold on?

'Ivan,' Edina said, 'is there any point in holding James Brodie? We know he hasn't got the reliquary.'

'Think, woman! Think! I need to know how much he has learned about our operation. Has he talked to anyone, eh?'

'I don't know,' Edina said.

'No, you don't. So I keep him locked up until I do know. I cannot finish him off until I know everything.' There was a pause. 'I have trouble with the monks. I punished them. I take their Father Abbot. I lock him up. But still they try to rebel.' Sikorsky sighed. 'Now I have trouble with the boy. Things are getting difficult. I think we leave soon.'

'Oh,' said Edina. 'I hadn't bargained on staying in Edinburgh for so short a time.'

'We move. We move. Always we move to stay ahead of the law,' said Sikorsky. 'You should know that well enough.'

'This isn't my fault,' said Edina.

'You should have control over your staff at the museum,' snapped Sikorsky. 'What were you thinking of letting her lend the reliquary to some writer, eh?'

'I was away. I . . .'

'You were CARELESS,' he yelled. 'Go back to the house and see if the young boy has hidden it, you stupid woman.'

Edina was clearly shaken. 'B . . . but you said Boyle and Butterworth have gone to Dean Terrace.'

'Those fools will find nothing. They are searching the street. But I don't believe the boy when he said he threw it out of the window. He is a liar. He has hidden it in the house, I think. Find it. Or is a child cleverer than you?'

'No . . . but I . . .'

He raised his hand but it stopped short of her cheek and he did not strike. He thought better of it and his hand fell to his side.

'Get back to your house and find it.'

'I thought I should wait for the consignment this evening.'

'You give me nothing but excuses. Go!'

Sikorsky spun round and marched back the way he had come. Edina hurried in the opposite direction without a word. Doors opened and slammed shut. There was silence once again.

As soon as Charlotte was certain she was alone, she slithered down the chimney, letting out a cry of pain as she fell. She dropped onto the hearth, shaking the soot from her clothes and licking the grazes on her hands. She had heard enough to know that both Dad and Harry were being held against their will and that she had to find them soon. If not, these criminals would most likely kill them both.

Quickly she pulled off her trainers and banged them against the side of the fireplace. Soot was clinging to the bottom of them and she had to be careful not to leave a trail of footprints behind her. Staying undetected and keeping out of sight in this place was not going to be easy.

With the trainers free of soot, she hurried towards the door at the far end which opened onto a cloistered area with doors leading off. Harry was locked up somewhere. She had heard them say so. But how was she going to find him?

23
The Great Escape

Charlotte stepped out into open cloisters and found the place deserted. Sikorsky and his men must be somewhere, she thought. She needed to be careful.

She passed through the cloisters, looking into every room — but she did not find Harry. It was only when she walked down a second corridor that she saw something that made her heart beat faster. Just inside a door was a metal trolley tipped on its side and nearby lay a pair of glasses. She bent down and picked them up. They were Harry's for sure. He must have been in this corridor. Maybe he wasn't far away. She slipped the glasses into the pocket of her jacket and continued her search until she came to a door that was smaller than the rest. It was old and wooden and studded with black metal nails.

Hoping she would find Harry at last, she turned the handle. The hinges creaked as the door opened but there was darkness on the other side. There were no windows. Nothing. She felt on the wall for a switch and found it. With the light of a single bulb, she saw a set of stone steps in front of her. They were steep and worn, leading into a dark hole. In different circumstances, Charlotte might have gone down to explore. But there was a terrible smell and, anyway, Harry wasn't there. Better get out before somebody came. She turned back towards the door.

It was then that she heard the voice.

'Oy! You!'

The voice echoed off the walls. She froze on the steps, not knowing where the voice was coming from. Should she run? Or was it already too late?

Then the voice came again.

'Who's up there? Get me out of here. I'm freezing!'

Now she recognized it. It was Harry.

Relief flooded over her. Then irritation.

'Shut up, you idiot,' she called. 'They'll hear you. I'm coming to get you out.'

'Charlie! How did you get . . .?'

'Shhhh. Don't make a noise. Just whisper. Where are you?'

'I'm in a sort of cupboard thing,' he hissed.

Charlotte hurried down the steps and across to the door at the end of the cellar. She tapped gently on it and whispered, 'You in here?'

''Course I'm in here,' Harry snapped. 'Where else would I be? It's disgusting. Get me out.'

Harry's lack of appreciation was typical. She leaned against the door, her arms folded. 'Maybe this is where you belong, bro. At least you can't get into any more trouble.'

'Big joke!' he replied. 'Now find the key, will you? It's here somewhere. Can you see it?'

Charlotte saw a row of hooks on the far wall with large metal keys hanging from them.

'There are lots,' she said and picked up several and walked back. The first one she tried didn't fit and neither did the second.

'Right. It has to be this one,' she said, putting the third key in the lock. This time it clicked and turned.

'Fantastic!' yelled Harry, pushing the door open. 'I'm out!' And he sprang like a baboon from the cupboard.

Charlotte was immediately struck by a nauseating smell. It filled her nostrils and mouth and, even though she covered her nose with her hand, she couldn't stop herself from retching.

'Yuk! That's one mega stink.'

'It's the primitive plumbing in there,' Harry explained and shut the cupboard door. 'That bucket's half full of you-know-what. They must have shut someone else in there recently.'

'Gross! Let's get out of this place. Quick.'

But they were too late. The door at the top of the steps creaked open.

'Back inside,' hissed Harry and they turned back towards the stinking cupboard. With their sweatshirts pulled over their noses, Harry and Charlotte squeezed inside and shut the door as quietly as they could.

'What's going on down there?' a rough voice called down. 'What's all the noise about?' It was LOVE HATE.

'I'm having a party,' Harry yelled back. 'You can come if you like.'

Heavy boots clanged as he came down the stone steps.

'Think you're clever, do yer?' he called. 'You need roughin' up, mate. A good seein' to will do you a world of good.'

'N . . . no,' said Harry. 'I'll be quiet, honest. I'll behave.'

LOVE HATE was outside the cupboard. 'Right then,' he said. 'I'll let it go this time. But you keep it shut or I'll have yer.'

He was about to leave when he spotted the key in

the lock. He frowned. Nobody should leave keys like that. They should hang them up. It was procedure. He knew the rules. As he reached out to remove the keys, he found that the door was unlocked. Now he was suspicious. He flung the cupboard door wide open and saw Charlotte crouching on the floor.

'Who's this, then?' he roared. 'How did you get in here, girl?'

But she didn't reply. She sprang out of the doorway. He tried to grab her but she dived round his legs and he missed. Charlotte jumped to her feet and ran for the steps, followed by LOVE HATE. But his monk's habit was long and heavy and it slowed him down. And when Harry flung the contents of the toilet bucket over the floor, it made it so slippery that LOVE HATE couldn't keep a foothold and he went crashing down, knocked senseless and left spread-eagled on the stone slabs.

'I never thought a bucket of pee would be so useful,' Harry laughed.

'Get him into the cupboard, quick,' said Charlotte and they both grabbed hold of his habit and dragged him along the floor like a great whale.

But he was too big to fit through the cupboard door.

'Bend his legs,' Harry insisted. 'We'll get him in somehow.'

With little resistance, they managed to fold him up like a piece of origami so that he fitted into that impossibly small space, unable to move. Although he wasn't tied up, he wouldn't have been able to move.

'Let's go,' Harry said. 'He'll start yelling and someone will come.'

But Charlotte knew how to stop him. She took off her trainer, whipped off her sock and stuffed it into his mouth.

Now he wouldn't be able to make much of a noise and it could be some time before anyone found him. No one would know that Harry had escaped or even that Charlotte was in the monastery. They wanted to keep it that way.

'We'll lock the door,' said Charlotte, 'and take the key with us. It'll take them ages to open it.'

'OK,' said Harry. 'Now let's get out of here and back to Edinburgh. I don't want to meet up with Sikorsky again.'

'Who?' asked Charlotte.

'The one who's in charge here,' said Harry. 'He's Russian, I think. A real thug.'

Then Charlotte thought back to when she had hidden in the chimney. 'I overheard him talking,' she said.

'Who?'

'Your Sicko or whatever he's called.'

'And?'

'They've got Dad and they're going to kill him. We can't leave, Harry. We've got to find Dad and get him out of here.'

24
Mistaken Identity

They hurried up the stone steps and into the silent corridor, letting the door swing shut behind them.

'Where now?' asked Harry. 'Where do you think they've put Dad?'

'I've no idea,' Charlotte replied. 'All we can do is search the building. Let's check it out.'

She pushed open a high oak door which revealed a deserted passageway stretching out in front of them.

More doors. Most of them were locked and so they tapped on them and pressed their ears against the wood, just in case Dad was inside. But there was never any response or sound of any movement. It was only when they were at the far end of the corridor that they found one door that wasn't locked.

'Careful,' said Charlotte as Harry turned the handle.

They found themselves in a square room which had been converted into a kitchen. There was a white sink under a high window, with an old gas cooker on the far wall and a fridge that was ten years old at least.

In the middle was a pine table with several mismatched chairs.

'Mmm,' said Charlotte. 'It could do with a lick of paint and some new units, don't you think?'

'This isn't Ideal Homes,' said Harry. 'When the monastery was built, the kitchen would have been in a separate building. Risk of fire and all that.'

'I know, I know,' Charlotte whispered. 'I do history too, remember.' She glanced quickly round the room. 'Well, Dad's obviously not in here. Let's go.'

Harry shook his head. 'I'm starving. I haven't eaten since breakfast. There must be something to eat in here.'

'We've got to go. Someone might come.'

Ignoring his sister, he went across to a large store cupboard and opened it to find shelves full of tins and packets of rice and pasta.

'No crisps – but they've got biscuits,' Harry said, pointing to the top shelf. Then he reached and grabbed hold of a packet of chocolate HobNobs.

'Stop messing, Harry. Come on!' Charlotte called.

Her brother looked round and grinned as he opened the packet. But his elbow caught a tin of beans and sent it toppling against another so that a whole row wobbled and cascaded off the shelf like lemmings leaping off a cliff. The noise as they crashed to the floor was deafening.

'Move!' hissed Charlotte. 'Now!'

But there was no time. A door next to the cupboard suddenly opened and a man in a monk's habit stood in the doorway. He was holding a knife and pointing it straight at Harry.

Harry froze, not daring to move.

'Who are you?' the monk asked.

'Who wants to know?' Harry replied, trying to sound tough even though his legs were shaking.

Then Charlotte chipped in. 'We've been drafted in from Edinburgh,' she lied. 'We came with Edina Ross this afternoon.'

The monk spun round to look at her. Now he was pointing the knife in her direction.

'Dear heaven!' he said. 'A girl?'

'Didn't they tell you we were coming?' Charlotte asked in her most grown-up voice.

'No,' the man replied. 'But why should they? They never tell us anything.' The hand holding the knife fell to his side and his shoulders drooped. 'I'd better get on with the cooking,' he said, walking towards the table. 'I take it there'll be two extra tonight.'

They noticed then that he was holding two onions

in the other hand. He placed them on the chopping board and began to slice them with the knife.

'We'll go,' said Harry, keen to be out of the way. Then, as he turned to leave, he paused. 'I don't suppose you know where we'll find the guy by the name of Brodie, do you? They brought him here earlier.'

The man didn't look up. 'No,' he said, as he chopped the onions.

'He's in his forties,' said Harry. 'Dark hair. They're holding him here.'

'I don't know anything.'

'Pity,' said Charlotte. 'We were told to go and talk to him – see if we could get anything out of him.'

The man looked up, shocked. He stopped slicing and rested his knife on the table. 'Tell me,' he said, fixing them with piercing blue eyes. 'What do youngsters like you get out of behaving like thugs? What is wrong with you? At your age, you should be full of life.'

Harry looked at Charlotte and she looked back at him. They didn't understand what they were hearing.

'How d'you mean "behaving like thugs"?' Harry asked.

The man sighed. 'Isn't that what you are? Thugs. You and Sikorsky's men? Intruding on us. Treating a

116

holy place as a convenience for your unlawful activities, whatever they are.'

Harry and Charlotte were trying to work it out. Who was this man?

'But *you're* one of Sikorsky's men,' Charlotte protested.

He clenched his fists, digging his nails into his palms, and looked at them in disgust. 'Do I look like one?'

'Anyone can wear a habit,' said Harry. 'It's a good disguise. Sikorsky's men wear habits.'

The monk shook his head. 'I wouldn't be one of his crooks if I were the last man on earth. No, I'd never be that. I am not like you. You chose to come here and work for a villain. I'm here because he won't let me leave.' He picked up his knife again and began frenzied chopping of the onions. 'Go,' he said. 'Do whatever you have to do and let me get on with my duties.'

25
Help At Last

'You're a monk, aren't you?' asked Charlotte. 'A real one?'

The monk, who was scarcely taller than Harry, raised his head. 'Well, I'm not one of your lot, that's for certain.'

Charlotte walked towards him. 'I'm sorry,' she said. 'I lied. We're not part of Sikorsky's gang. They kidnapped my brother and I found him in the cellar. Now we need to get out of here.'

Harry butted in. 'Except we can't go. They've still got our dad somewhere and we've got to find him.'

The monk sank down onto one of the chairs, pulled out a handkerchief and wiped his forehead.

'Maybe you can help us,' said Harry.

The monk leaned forward and lowered his voice as if he was afraid of being overheard. 'With all my heart, I will try,' he said. 'But you've put yourselves in real danger. I think you'd better come with me.'

He stood up and beckoned the children to follow him out of the kitchen and down the corridor.

'We are safe here,' the monk said, opening a door into a makeshift dormitory where metal-framed beds were crammed together like some kind of prison camp.

'As long as we behave ourselves, they leave us alone. This is the only room where we can be private – even though we are packed like sardines.'

Charlotte and Harry sat on the edge of the nearest bed while the monk told them what had happened.

'I am Brother Michael and I am one of eight monks who lived here peacefully until Ivan Sikorsky arrived like some deadly plague.' His voice shook with anger. 'At first we welcomed him – we didn't know him for the evil man he is. Then his men arrived and it became obvious that he intended to carry out criminal activities. Of course, we asked him to leave.'

'But he wouldn't go?'

'He threatened us. He said that if we didn't co-operate, we would regret it. If we contacted anyone . . . if we tried to escape . . .'

'What?'

Brother Michael bowed his head. 'At first we resisted but they threatened us with guns,' he said. 'And, as punishment, they burned our books. Our marvellous, precious old books.'

'That's gross,' said Charlotte.

Brother Michael nodded, twisting his bony hands over and over before he spoke. 'Some of us tried to escape on the horses but they drove after us and it didn't take long to catch us.'

'What did they do?'

'They fenced us in like cattle. And worse. They took our dear Father Abbot and they are still holding him, just like your father. They say they will kill him if we attempt another escape or make contact with the police.' The monk closed his eyes, shaking his head from side to side. 'We cannot risk it. We pray every day that they will not stay long.' Then he blew his nose and wiped a tear from his cheek.

'But what's Sicko-what's-his-name doing here?' asked Charlotte. 'Why did he come?'

'It's obvious,' said Harry. 'It's got to be something to do with the reliquary. Illegal diamond smuggling. And somehow it's connected with the museum.'

Brother Michael sighed. '*We* don't know what's going on. All we see are cardboard boxes but . . .'

They heard footsteps in the corridor and Brother Michael became agitated.

'I'm sorry,' he said. 'I must go back to the kitchen or I'll be missed. You stay here. No one will come into the dormitory except the brothers. You are safe.'

'But we've got to find Dad,' said Harry. 'We can't wait . . .'

Brother Michael held up his hand. 'Please. Let me help. As soon as I find out anything about your father, I'll be back.'

He left them to return to his cooking and Harry slumped miserably on the bed. Charlotte leaned towards him and pushed her nose into his face. 'Hey, gloomy boy. Don't be so miserable. We've got help coming, right?'

Harry shrugged.

'Anyway, I've got a present for you, bro. Not that you deserve it. But then I'm an amazing and utterly kind sister.'

'What are you on about?'

Charlotte felt in her jacket pocket and pulled out the glasses she had found in the corridor. 'They're a bit cracked but they're better than nothing, eh?'

'Great,' he said and hooked them over his ears. 'What's one crack when I've got two lenses?'

They sat together, side by side on the iron-framed bed. 'Edina's gone back to Edinburgh,' said Charlotte. 'Sicko insisted she went and checked out the house again to see if the reliquary was there. I heard them talking.'

121

'She'll be two hours, at least,' said Harry. 'It depends how long it takes her to find the reliquary. Where did you put it after I threw it out of the window?'

'In my saddlebag,' Charlotte said.

Harry looked crestfallen. 'Then we're done for. Boyle and Butterworth have gone back to Dean Terrace to search in the street.'

'The street? Why are they doing that?'

Harry hung his head and bit nervously at his thumb nail. ''Cos I told them I'd thrown it out of the bedroom window.'

Charlotte sat up. 'You did WHAT?'

'I know,' said Harry. 'But I couldn't help it. You've never been beaten up by a crazy psycho. I tell you – you'd say anything to stop the pain.'

Charlotte rested her hand on his shoulder. 'If it makes you feel any better, Harry, I don't think they'll find my bike or the reliquary.'

Harry brightened. 'You don't?'

'No. I hid it on the other side of the road. My bike's under a great weeping willow. They'll never see it.'

'Good thinking, sis,' said Harry, grinning broadly. 'Did you hide my bike, too?'

'No. It should still be leaning on the railing outside Edina Ross's house, where you left it.'

Harry's jaw dropped and he stared at his sister, his eyes growing round as golf balls. 'I don't believe it. You mean you left my brand new bike out there? You idiot! What did you do that for?'

His bike – the Raleigh Motomax FS with eighteen-speed twist-grip gears – was his most prized possession. Every boy's dream machine. No wonder he went ballistic when he learned that his sister had abandoned it to every thief in Edinburgh.

'Don't lose your rag, bro,' said Charlotte, holding up her hands. 'What else could I do? I was too busy hiding in the back of the Jag to think about your bike.'

Harry sighed heavily and then reluctantly said, 'Suppose so.'

'Just think about it,' she said. 'Boyle and Butterworth will find your bike but they won't find the reliquary, will they?'

'They will if they do find *your* bike, stupid!'

'And why would they go looking for mine? They don't even know I went with you. They think you went to see Edina on your own.'

'True.'

'So, once we get out of here, we'll still have the reliquary as evidence. Trust me.'

Time seemed to pass slowly. They sat on the edge of the beds waiting for Brother Michael to return.

Charlotte suddenly jumped to her feet. 'I'm an idiot.'

'I've known that for years,' said Harry.

'No, listen,' she said, feeling in the side pockets of her jeans. 'I can't believe I didn't think of it earlier.'

'What?'

'My mobile. All we've got to do is phone the police. They'll be here in no time. We can tell them what we know about Sicko and then the brothers will tell them the rest.'

'Right. Do it. They'll find us. There can't be too many monasteries within an hour of Edinburgh.'

But Charlotte's expression had changed from excitement to one of disbelief. 'It's not there,' she said.

'Try your other pockets,' said Harry.

'I have. All three. It's gone. I must have dropped it.'

'Where?'

'I don't know, do I? How would I know?'

'Think, Charlie, think!'

Charlotte wiped her hand across her forehead. 'The last time I had it,' she said, 'was when I rang you at Edina Ross's house.'

This was not the time for Harry to point out how

disastrous that stupid phone call had been for him. He would leave that conversation until later.

'So *where* did you put it? You *can't* just lose it. Nobody just loses their mobile. Stop being such a cretin.'

'Don't bully me!' snapped Charlotte. 'I put it in my pocket. I know I did.'

'Well, it's not there now, is it? Brilliant!'

They sat in silence except for the sound of deep sighs and Harry grinding his teeth. After some time, he got up and began pacing the room. He was desperate for action. Where was Brother Michael? When were they going to do something?

He wagged his finger at Charlotte. 'You know, once Boyle and Butterworth get back, it's all over. Dad will be in serious danger. It's no good, Charlie. Time's running out.'

And then the door opened.

26
Action Gets Results

They spun round and stared. It was not Brother Michael. They had been careless and caught off-guard. They gawped at the tall, skinny man in the doorway. They couldn't tell who it was under the black habit. They held their breath, waiting for him to speak. Anxious to know whether he was on their side or the enemy's.

Those seconds seemed like hours. The man stepped inside, turned and closed the door behind him. 'I have come from Brother Michael,' he said in a nervous, high-pitched voice. 'I have news.'

The twins breathed again and the monk continued. 'Yesterday, I overheard one of Ivan Sikorsky's men talking and I'm certain that your father is being held in one of the upstairs rooms.'

'What are we going to do then?' Harry asked.

'When the brothers return from the fields, we have a plan to help you get him out.'

'Great,' said Harry. 'Let's go.'

The monk shook his head. 'We can do nothing until

this evening, I'm afraid. During the day we are constantly watched by Sikorsky's men.'

'We can't wait,' said Harry.

'You must. They know everything we do in the daytime. If we are caught helping you, our Father Abbot will suffer. They have threatened to kill him, you know.' He glanced nervously at the door. 'I'm sorry. I must go now.' He opened the door a fraction and peered into the corridor to check that it was clear. Then he raised his hand in a silent goodbye and walked out.

Harry's impatience was at boiling point. There was no way that he could stay in a cramped little room, knowing that Dad was somewhere upstairs. He would explode.

'If he thinks we're going to wait here all afternoon,' he said. 'He's got another think coming.'

'They're going to help us,' said Charlotte, trying to calm him down.

'Well, I think there are things we can do for ourselves. Think about it, Charlie. The place is practically deserted – so how would anyone see us? I don't believe a word that monk said. Come on. We're not going to hang around.'

Charlotte agreed that time was running out. 'OK,'

she said. 'We'll do it. We'll try the front of the monastery. That's the most likely place. I saw a row of bedroom windows over the front door. Dad could be up there.'

'Right then,' said Harry. 'Let's go.'

To get back to the stairs, they had to pass Sikorsky's study and go down the corridor past the abandoned metal trolley.

'You should have seen me on that, Charlie,' Harry said, pointing to the trolley. 'I was brilliant! It was like that film *The Great Escape* except I wasn't on a motorbike. I used that trolley like a giant skateboard.'

'What happened?'

'My progress was stopped by a door.'

When they arrived at the entrance hall, they went up the stairs two at a time to the first floor where the passageway turned sharply left and stretched the length of the building. There were five doors.

The first one was locked but when they opened the second and stepped into the room, they saw a shirt and dirty underpants abandoned on an unmade bed. There was a stink of cigarettes and cheap aftershave.

'This isn't Dad's stuff,' Charlotte said, glancing round. 'Come on. Let's go.'

Before they left the room, they heard a noise, muffled

and indistinct but not far away. They stood still. Charlotte glanced at Harry, her eyes wide with fear, wondering if they were about to be discovered. Harry held up his hands and shrugged – not sure either.

Another noise.

Charlotte dropped to her knees and poked her head out of the door at low level. The corridor was empty.

Cautiously, they tiptoed out. Then the noise came again, louder this time, and they realized it was coming from the next room.

Harry pointed to the door. 'The key's in the lock,' he hissed. 'Somebody forgot it.'

'Suppose one of Sicko's men is inside,' whispered Charlotte.

'Or not,' said Harry, leaning forward and pressing his ear to the door. 'I can hear a sort of groaning.'

'Try the key,' Charlotte suggested.

Harry turned it and there was an audible click.

'It was locked, Charlie. They've locked somebody in there.'

'It might be Dad!' said Charlotte.

Harry looked at his sister and put his finger to his lips. Then slowly he pressed the handle, pushed the door open and stepped into a darkened room. Heavy curtains were drawn over the window and, at first, they could see nothing. Only when their eyes became adjusted to the lack of light were they able to see the shadowy outline of a bed and someone lying on it.

Cautiously, Charlotte stepped across the room to the bed. She knelt down and looked at the person on it. Through the gloom, she could just make out that it was a man. She dared to lift her hand and touch his hair with the lightest touch so as not to wake him.

Her heartbeat quickened. What if it was *not* Dad?

She ran her fingers over his cheek. Down to his chin. She turned and grabbed Harry's arm.

'It's Dad!' she whispered. 'I'd know his face anywhere. Shut the door, and turn the light on, will you?'

Harry took the key out of the lock, shut the door and locked it from the inside so that no one would be able to get in. Smart thinking. Then he switched on the light.

Dad moaned, covering his eyes with his arm to block out the light and shifted his position so that he lay on his side. The bed was just a bare mattress with no sheets to cover him. Close by there were three chairs as if people had been sitting round watching him.

Charlotte bent over him. 'Dad,' she whispered. 'Dad, it's me, Charlotte.'

He moved a little and groaned as if it hurt to move. He didn't open his eyes.

'Dad, come on. Wake up. We've come to get you out of here.'

His eyelids suddenly shot open and he stared directly at her. 'Leave me alone,' he said in a thick, sleepy voice. 'I don't know anything. I've told you.'

As he turned, she saw that one side of his face was purple with bruising. There was a deep cut on his forehead and his cheek was grazed and encrusted with dried blood.

'Let me try and wake him,' said Harry, stepping forward and pushing Charlotte to one side. 'Dad, it's Harry. Are you OK?' and he reached out to shake his shoulder.

This time, Dad slowly opened his eyes and recognized his son standing by the bed. 'Harry,' he said. Then Charlotte took hold of his hand and he looked at her. 'Charlotte. I don't understand. What are you doing here?'

'We're going to get you out of this place, Dad,' Charlotte said. 'Don't worry.'

Their father was confused. He shook his head from side to side as if to clear his befuddled mind.

'We know all about the reliquary, Dad,' said Harry.

'We found it yesterday. But it's safe. We're going to take it to the police when we get away from here.'

Dad closed his eyes. 'That's what all this trouble is about. That reliquary. Those diamonds. I should have gone to the police straightaway. But . . . the museum . . . I thought Edina should know. I had to tell her I'd found the diamonds.'

'No, Dad. She—'

'I tried to contact her, you know.' Dad's voice was almost inaudible now as if he was talking in his sleep. 'Her mobile was switched off. All I could do was leave a message. Edina would have known what to do. But it was too late. Too late. Those thugs got to me . . .'

Charlotte sat on the bed. 'Dad,' she said gently. 'Listen. Edina isn't our friend. Edina is part of all this.'

Harry nodded. 'I bet she rang Sikorsky as soon as she got your message, Dad. They're in this together. Making loads of dosh.'

Dad closed his eyes as if unable to bear what he was hearing. So it had come to this. His old friend was a criminal. And he never guessed.

'Honest, Dad,' Harry continued. 'This Russian

called Sikorsky has got a whole bunch of thugs working for him. There's this one with tattoos on and . . .'

Charlotte nudged him to shut up. 'Don't worry, Dad,' she said, stroking his forehead. 'We've got a plan to get us out of here.'

27
A Piece of Luck

Charlotte looked at her watch, then she looked at Harry.

'There's not much time,' she said. 'Edina could be back in an hour and a half. Sikorsky will go mad when he knows she hasn't found the reliquary.'

'True,' said Harry. 'Let's get moving.'

'I'm going back downstairs to find Brother Michael,' she said. 'I'll tell him we've found Dad.'

'OK,' Harry said. 'I agree. We'll do that.'

'No. *I'll* do it. *You* have to stay here.'

'No way!'

'I know the layout of the monastery better than you.'

Harry grunted. He didn't want to stay. He liked to be in on the action.

'I'm going,' said Charlotte. 'I'll lock the door. Get Dad to drink plenty of water.' She pointed to a sink in the corner. 'That'll help him to wake up properly. I won't be long.'

She closed the door behind her, turned the key in

the lock and put it in her pocket. She hurried down the staircase but as she reached the bottom, she heard voices along the corridor. Men were shouting and there was the sound of running feet. She could only think of one reason. Sikorsky had found out that Harry had escaped and had sent his men to look for him.

Quickly, Charlotte slipped into the darkness of the space under the stairs and stayed very still while three men in black habits ran past, panting heavily. They ran out through the main door shouting to each other and the last one left it wide open. Charlotte stayed where she was, crouched and listening.

How long should she wait? she wondered. She was terrified of being discovered. But the voices and the sound of running feet faded and she dared to come out of her hiding place. The corridor was empty. Thank goodness. She hurried through the cloisters and had almost reached the kitchen when she heard something that made her pulse race. Sikorsky was in a nearby room talking – no, shouting – into a phone.

'What you mean, "problems"?' he yelled. 'You say you come, no?'

Through the open door, his voice was deafening and his accent was stronger than ever. He screamed and thumped his desk after each word. 'You come tonight or you pay. You pay.'

Charlotte stood outside, afraid to pass the open door. She didn't know what to do. Should she risk being seen or go back upstairs? She didn't have a choice.

She walked on, making as little noise as possible. One step, two, three . . . past the door.

At that very moment, Sikorsky slammed the telephone down on the desk. Charlotte heard him push his chair back and his heavy footsteps came stomping towards the doorway. He would see her for sure. All she could do was press her back against the wall hoping he would walk the other way down the corridor. If he didn't, she would run like crazy.

Sikorsky stormed out of the office in a furious temper. He shouted for his men but his voice echoed along the empty corridor. No one was there to answer. Luckily for Charlotte, the Russian turned right and didn't see her standing rock still and wild eyed. She let out a heavy sigh. She was safe for a little while longer.

As she stepped away from the wall, she saw that Sikorsky had left the door of the office open and there, on the desk, was a large old telephone.

28
All Stuck Up

If I'm quick, Charlotte thought, I can call for help.

It was dangerous. It was daring. But she thought there was a chance that she could pull it off. Sikorsky had disappeared into the cloisters so she took her chance. She closed the door of the office, ran behind the desk and picked up the heavy old phone. Then she dialled 999.

A woman answered almost immediately. 'Which service do you require?'

'Police,' Charlotte whispered.

'Please give me your name and address.'

Charlotte groaned. Too slow. Too slow.

'My name is Charlotte Brodie and . . .'

'How old are you, Charlotte?'

'What does it matter?'

'I'm here to help you, Charlotte. Are you alone?'

'Not exactly.'

'Then where are you?'

'I . . . I'm not sure.'

'Do you have a parent there with you or—'

'Yes, but—'

'No need to be afraid, Charlotte. Just tell me where you are and a police car will be on its way in no time at all. Just give me the address, please.'

'I can't give you the address. I don't know what it is.'

It was at this point that she heard a noise in the corridor. Footsteps. Voices. Sikorsky was coming back. She grabbed the phone, set it on the floor behind the desk and knelt down beside it.

'Charlotte, are you there?' The woman's voice came out of the receiver.

'Yes,' she whispered.

'Please speak up, I can hardly hear you.'

'I can't,' she whispered, wrapping her hand around the mouthpiece.

'I'm sorry—'

Just then, Charlotte heard the footsteps stop in the doorway to the study. She daren't say another word. Instead, she put the receiver back slowly, slowly – careful not to make a noise – and she wriggled into the kneehole of the desk, lying as still as stone, jammed into the small space, hardly daring to breathe. She crossed her fingers, squeezed her eyes tight shut and waited.

'What do you mean, you can't find him?' Sikorsky yelled as he flung open the door. 'He must be here somewhere. He has his duties. You find him. I have no time. I am very busy man.'

Sikorsky slammed the door, leaving the other man outside in the corridor, and marched across to the desk.

It was all up for Charlotte.

When she dared to open her eyes just a fraction, she saw his feet half a metre away. What silly shoes. Black patent leather. Expensive with built-up heels to make him look taller, she guessed.

Sikorsky spoke again, this time to himself. 'What is that?' He sounded puzzled and irritated at the same time and Charlotte realized that he had seen the phone on the floor. Any minute now he would bend down to pick it up and he would see her under the desk. She was desperate. She had to do something. Anything.

She did the only thing she could think of. She reached out and grabbed hold of his ankle. She tugged violently so that Sikorsky was taken by surprise and tipped off balance and his great bulk toppled backwards. His arms flailed as he tried to stop himself from falling but he crashed against the wall, banging his head on the filing cabinet and slithering to the floor.

There was good news.

There was bad news.

The good news was that Sikorsky was unconscious and wouldn't be able to call for help. The bad news was that he was pressed against the kneehole of the desk so that Charlotte couldn't get out. His great belly was blocking her escape.

She knew she must push him out of the way. He might wake up at any moment. But it was like trying to move an elephant. She couldn't do it. She tried again. And again she failed.

In one final effort, she took a deep breath, pressed her back against the underside of the desk and rammed her hands against his side. Then she gritted her teeth and pushed with all her strength. This time his bloated body slid just a little way – but it was enough to leave a space big enough for her to wriggle out and clamber over him.

Relieved that she was free, she stood up and looked around the room. Somehow, she had to tie him up. But what could she use? She didn't have a rope. Nothing. On the far end of the desk behind a laptop, she saw a large metal tape dispenser. Quickly she picked it up and put it on the floor next to Ivan Sikorsky's head. She pulled on the sticky tape and wrapped it round and round his mouth until he looked like one of those

Egyptian mummies she had seen in books. With his mouth well and truly covered, he wouldn't be able to make much noise when he woke up.

Next, she grabbed hold of his hands and wrapped more of the sticky tape around them. It would be difficult for him to move at all now. Excellent.

Charlotte felt pleased with herself. Job well done. But suddenly Sikorsky gave a long, low groan as he began to wake up. Someone would hear for sure. Even with the tape over his mouth, the groans were quite loud. It wouldn't be long before someone came in to see what the noise was about.

She looked around the room for something to cover him with. Over on a stand in the corner hung a thick black overcoat. It was exactly right. She lifted it off the hook and threw it over Sikorsky's head. When he groaned for a second time, she was satisfied that the sound was so muffled that no one outside the room would hear.

Time to ring the police again. She hoped they wouldn't ask stupid questions this time. It was an emergency. She needed them to come at once.

She looked for the phone. It was large and had once been white but over the years had turned yellow. It was practically an antique. She finally found it on the other side of the desk. It must have been kicked there when Sikorsky fell. She reached for the receiver and pressed it to her ear. But there was no dialling tone. It was dead. She glanced down at the cord and saw that it had been wrenched from the back of the receiver during the struggle. An old phone. A rotten cord. No surprise that it had broken.

It was Charlotte's turn to groan. What now? She had to find Brother Michael, he would know what to do. She stepped over Sikorsky's prostrate body, ready to leave and, as she did, she glanced at the laptop on the desk. It must be Sikorsky's. Monks didn't go in for hi-tech stuff. Charlotte looked at the screen and read the email that was open.

Collection at 2030. This time Morgan's Point. No waiting or back to Rotterdam. Problems with Revenue and Customs. Cash as agreed.

Next to the laptop was a road atlas, open at a map of Scotland. Someone had drawn a circle in black felt pen on the coast to the north-east of Edinburgh and had written the initials MP next to it. And the letter M had been written a little distance away. MP for Morgan's Point? M for monastery? Something was going to happen tonight at half past eight. She glanced at her watch. It was quarter to five.

She tore the page from the road atlas, folded it and pushed it into a pocket, ready to show it to Brother Michael. Maybe he would know what it was all about.

She walked away from the desk, opened the door into the silent corridor and hurried to the high oak door. She was about to open it when she heard a man speak on the other side. She pressed her back to the wall hoping that if he opened the door he wouldn't see her. She stood there rigid and listened.

'He's in the study, Miss Ross,' he said. 'Just go straight in.'

Charlotte's pulse raced. Could Edina Ross be back already? She would be sure to find Sikorsky and then all hell would break loose. There was no time to look for Brother Michael. It was imperative that they got Dad away and hid him somewhere where Sikorsky would never find him.

29
Hide-and-Seek

Edina Ross knocked on the study door before stepping inside.

She stared at the empty room. 'That's annoying,' she said to Boyle and Butterworth who were standing behind her. 'After rushing back from Edinburgh, Ivan's not here.'

Their visit to Dean Terrace had been a complete waste of time. Butterworth and Boyle had searched the road and pavement outside Edina's house while Edina had enlisted the help of Mrs McFee to check the rooms. They had failed to find the reliquary.

Boyle folded his arms across his chest and said, 'Well, I'm not bothered where Mr Sikorsky is. I don't want to be the one to tell him we haven't found that box thingy. Sure, he'll go stark raving mad, I know it. He's got a temper on him worse than me dad.'

Edina Ross raised an eyebrow and gave Boyle a withering look.

'I expect he's out in the grounds,' she said. 'I don't

know what's going on there but I saw some of the men running around like headless chickens. I'll go and find out what they're up to.'

She stepped back to leave the study, which was unfortunate for Boyle as he was standing directly behind and her high stiletto heel pierced his trainer and punctured his foot, sending him into howling hysterics.

'AAAAAAAAGHH!' he screamed as he lunged across the room. 'AAAAAAAAGHH!' he yelled again. 'Me toes! Me foot! AAAAAAAAGHH!'

Wailing and bawling, Boyle perched on the desk hugging his injury. It was as he was wiping the blood off his toes that he saw something out of the corner of his eye. His eyes grew as big as gobstoppers as he realized that Ivan Sikorsky was lying on the floor trussed up like an oven-ready turkey. Boyle couldn't speak. Instead he made strange gurgling sounds in his throat and raised his hand to point at the space behind the desk.

'What now?' Edina snapped.

'Pull yourself together, man,' said Butterworth. 'It's just a scratch.'

But Boyle's eyes were fixed on the prostrate Russian. 'It . . . it's . . . it's him,' he said at last.

'Somebody's done him over. Dear to goodness! Just look at him.'

Butterworth and Edina went over to the desk.

'What are you talking about?' Edina asked. But when she leaned over and saw Sikorsky's shoes sticking out from under a black overcoat, she panicked.

'Ivan!' she said, racing round the desk and crouching over him. 'Are you all right?' She pulled the coat off him. 'What on earth . . .?' The sight of his face covered in sticky tape made her squeal. She clapped one hand over her mouth and pointed at Sikorsky with the other. His eyes were open wide and glowering with fury.

'Get that tape off,' she shouted hysterically. 'Quick! Get it off! Get it off!'

Butterworth pushed Boyle off the desk. 'You heard the lady. Remove the tape.'

'But I . . .' Boyle began.

'Do it!' Butterworth insisted.

Boyle shook his head. 'Me foot hurts,' he said.

Butterworth raised his hand and clouted him across his head, propelling him towards the bloated body of his boss.

'Right then,' said Boyle, taking a deep breath before bending over. 'Right then,' he said again and gripped the end of the sticky tape.

Sikorsky's eyes grew wild, knowing what was to come. He tried to speak but the only noise he could make was 'Mmmmmmm, mmmmmmm'.

'Don't you worry, Mr Sikorsky,' said Boyle. 'I'll have this stuff off in no time at all. Clean as a whistle.' Then, in one vicious swoop, he ripped the tape away from Sikorsky's face, taking skin and hair with it.

'Aaaaaaaaaaaaaggggggggggggghhhhhhhh!' he screamed, turning scarlet with pain and rage. 'What are you doing? Aaaaaagghhh! You stupid man. Aaaaaagghhh! That is agony! Aaaaaagghhh!'

Butterworth shoved Boyle roughly to one side. 'Leave it to me, boss,' he said. 'I'll be gentle as a lamb. I'll have the rest off before you know it.'

'Then do it!' snapped Sikorsky. 'Get this stuff off my hands. But if you don't do better . . .'

Butterworth immediately regretted stepping into Boyle's shoes. Sikorsky glared at him with such fury that his hands began to tremble and it took him twice as long to cut through the tape. When the Russian was finally free, he gave an exasperated growl and grabbed hold of Butterworth so that he could heave himself off the floor. Then he flopped into the chair behind the desk and sat there, panting.

Edina placed her hand on his shoulder. 'You poor, poor man,' she said.

But Sikorsky knocked it away, peevishly. He was irritated and deeply embarrassed at being bound and gagged in his own study. 'I did not see who did this,' he snapped.

'You didn't?' she said.

'How could I? He was lying in wait under the desk. It was a complete surprise. He was very strong. Very strong.'

Edina Ross paused to think.

'Surely it couldn't be James Brodie or his son. You have them locked up, don't you?'

Sikorsky gave a sharp intake of breath as he realized. 'It could only be the boy,' he said. 'It must have been him. Cunning little worm.' His eyes flashed with anger as he pointed towards Boyle and Butterworth. 'You were supposed to lock him up, idiots.'

Butterworth nodded frantically. Then Boyle, who was standing behind him, said, 'Sure I locked the door myself, I did. Down in that cellar place. The one where the old monks used to keep their milk and . . .'

Sikorsky waved his hand to silence him and, as a final insult, Butterworth dug him in the ribs.

'Go and check the cellar,' Sikorsky barked. 'See that he is still there.'

The two men rushed out of the door, glad to be away from their boss. Today had been the worst day they could remember. It surely couldn't get worse.

30
The Pink Mobile

Sikorsky leaned forward in his chair, his black eyes directed at Edina. 'So. You have found the reliquary in your house, yes?'

Her reply was almost inaudible. 'Not exactly,' she said.

'Is that yes or no?' he growled.

Edina Ross shook her head nervously. 'I'm afraid I don't have it.'

There was a sudden explosion of Sikorsky's temper. His face turned from white to red to purple and he thumped his fist on the desk. 'Why am I surrounded by fools?'

Edina held up her hands as if to defend herself. 'I searched every room. Every cupboard. And Boyle and Butterworth looked out in the road and there was nothing but—'

'BUT? BUT? What "but" can there be?'

'I think I have found an explanation.'

He leaned back in his chair and narrowed his eyes. 'I hope this will be interesting,' he said.

Edina shifted, her nerves on edge. 'I found something in the back of my car,' she said.

'Oh, you found something in your car,' he said sarcastically. 'And what has that to do with the reliquary?'

She swallowed as she explained. 'It was a mobile phone. Pink. I've seen it before.'

'A pink mobile phone,' Sikorsky mocked. 'I must say that is of NO interest to me.'

'But I'm certain it belonged to the boy's sister. I believe she stole a ride in the back of my car this morning and that's when she dropped it.'

The Russian gripped the desk with both hands. 'The boy has a *sister*? And you never told me? The boy has a sister who *came here in your car*?' He raised his fists and shook them at the ceiling. 'Why you not tell me the boy had a sister? WHY? WHY? WHY?'

Edina tried to control her nerves but failed. 'H-Harry and his s-sister came to my house yesterday to show me the reliquary. But only the boy came this morning to get it back. He said Charlotte – that's his sister – had gone to her auntie's.'

'And you believed him?' shouted Sikorsky.

Edina nodded.

'So you let her into your car? Is that what you did?'

'I didn't know she was there.'

'Oh, so you didn't know?' he sneered. 'And now she has come to the monastery, huh?'

Before Sikorsky could start shouting again, the door burst open and Boyle and Butterworth rushed into the study, panting. They were followed by LOVE HATE who filled the room with the stink of pee.

'They did 'im over, sir,' said Boyle, nodding towards LOVE HATE. 'He put up a real fight, I tell yer, but the boy's gone.'

Sikorsky's blood pressure was now at danger point. The veins in his temple were throbbing as if they were about to burst.

'GONE? How? The boy was locked up, was he not? How could he escape from that cellar? How could he win a fight with a grown man like you?'

'I was overcome,' said LOVE HATE, shifting from one foot to the other. 'It wasn't just the boy. There were two of 'em. A girl as well. They tricked me, boss.' He hung his head, embarrassed. 'They locked me up.'

The Russian gritted his teeth and then banged his fist so hard on the desk that the pens and paper, even the laptop, bounced on the surface. 'And I now know that this girl is the boy's sister,' he said, glaring at Edina Ross. 'It was she who set the boy free, huh?'

Edina tried to stay calm. 'I am almost certain that the boy threw the reliquary down to his sister from my bedroom window. She was probably in the street.'

Sikorsky gripped her arm. 'So it was the girl who took it. Then we must find her. If she is here, she can't go far. She will tell us where she has hidden it.'

'They could be on their way to the village,' Edina suggested. 'They might be on their way to get help.'

'You think I let anyone leave this place, huh?' he mocked. 'The fence is electrified. It will keep them both inside the grounds, I think. Unless they want to find out what a thousand volts of electricity feels like.'

Sikorsky stood up from his desk and turned to Boyle, Butterworth and LOVE HATE. 'You go out and find them. NOW!'

31
Escape or Die

Now that Edina was back, Charlotte knew that it wouldn't be long before she discovered Sikorsky behind the desk. No point in hanging around. She must hurry back to Harry and get Dad out of that room. Before long, the Russian would find out that Harry had escaped and his gang of thugs would come looking for him. She scurried through the ground floor constantly on the alert. If she was seen, it would be over – for all of them.

She had almost reached the staircase when she heard footsteps – men running in her direction. She flung herself in the darkness under the stairs where she crouched and waited. The footsteps came nearer. The men arrived and stopped at the foot of the stairs. Charlotte could almost touch them. But they failed to see her in the shadows.

She noticed that Boyle, who was last to arrive, was limping badly and was so out of breath that he leaned forward with his hands on his knees panting and gasping for air.

LOVE HATE stood in front of the group and took charge. 'You two,' he said, pointing to the younger men. 'Go and fetch Brodie. Quick as you can.'

'From upstairs?'

'Where did you think?' he jeered. 'In the rose garden?'

The men looked away, their heads bowed, but said nothing.

'The boss wants him right now,' LOVE HATE continued. 'He's going to ask him a few questions. Have a nice little chat.' And he laughed. 'Very nice.'

Charlotte felt sick. If they found Dad she didn't dare to think what they would do.

'What about the rest of us?' Butterworth asked. 'What do you want us to do?'

'We'll search the grounds for the kid and his sister. A boy and a girl. Got that?'

Charlotte was depressed to hear that. So they know I'm here, she said to herself. That made things worse. Much worse.

The group of men split. Two went upstairs and the rest ran outside. But Charlotte knew she had a few minutes in which she could act. When the two men found that the door to Dad's bedroom was locked, they would go to fetch another key. That would give her a very short time to get Harry and Dad out of the room.

But how?

The staircase was out of bounds, she knew. One of the thugs might see her. There was only one way to get Dad out of the building and that was dangerous. But it was possible.

When she was sure that Sikorsky's men had gone, she sneaked out through the front door. She turned to the right, then, pressing her back to the wall, she sidestepped until she was directly under the room where Dad and Harry were waiting. She looked up at the window that was going to be their escape route.

Immediately to the left of the bedroom, the building jutted out. Charlotte was pleased to see that there was a drainpipe running down at the junction of the two walls. Not only that, the stone wall was covered in thick ivy which was probably as old as the monastery itself and would be strong enough to support them as they climbed down from the window. The drainpipe and the ivy. That should be enough. Charlotte hoped so.

She bent down and picked a pebble off the ground and hurled it at the window. She waited but nothing happened. She picked two larger ones and flung them as hard as she could . . . one . . . two . . .

The window was thrown open and Harry looked out.

'It's me,' she called up as quietly as she could.

'You nearly broke the window, you idiot,' he shouted back.

'Sssssh!'

'Well, why didn't you come up the stairs?' said Harry, lowering his voice.

'No time to explain. You've got to get out of there.'

Harry shrugged. 'How do I do that? You've got the key.'

'Climb down the drainpipe.'

He shook his head violently. 'No way.'

'You'll have to. They're coming any minute now. I overheard them.'

Harry disappeared inside and was gone for what seemed like ages. Charlotte guessed he was talking to Dad, trying to convince him that he had to climb down a drainpipe or some old ivy and risk plummeting to the ground. Tricky choice.

When Harry reappeared at the window, he called, 'OK. We'll give it a go – but I think this is crazy. Honestly, sis, I think you could have come up with a better idea.'

When Dad came to the window, Charlotte was pleased to see that he was looking more alert and more like his old self, almost awake. He leaned out and waved down to her.

'There's a drainpipe to your right,' she called up. 'Hold onto that, Dad, and use the stems of the ivy as you climb down.'

'I'll go first,' called Harry.

It was a piece of luck that the drainpipe was made of cast iron and not plastic and it was near enough to the window for them to grab hold of.

Charlotte muttered under her breath, 'Please let the drainpipe be strong enough. And please don't let anyone see them. Pleeeeeease.'

Harry turned his back to the window and wriggled through the opening until his legs were hanging over the windowsill with his feet dangling in mid air. He swung one leg to the left, trying to gain a foothold on the ivy and, when his toes finally found a strong stem, he took his left hand off the sill and reached across to the drainpipe and grabbed it.

'Here I go!' he said.

Charlotte hardly dared to look. Her brother had to put all his trust in the strength of the drainpipe. She suddenly wondered if the fixings that held it to the wall were OK. What if they had corroded with age? Rusted? Rotted and weakened? She clapped her hands over her eyes and counted, one . . . two . . . three . . . praying that she wouldn't hear a scream or a thud or a crash as Harry fell.

But no. Instead, she suddenly felt a hand on her shoulder. She stopped breathing and froze on the spot. She turned and dared to open her eyes. There was Harry standing in front of her grinning broadly.

'Don't do that!' she squealed, pounding his chest with both fists. 'You terrified me.'

Her brother pushed her away. 'OK, sis. No worries. That climb was a piece of cake for me,' he said.

'What about Dad?'

Harry frowned and shook his head. 'Listen,' he said. 'Dad won't be able to do it. He's still shaky.'

'Then what . . .?'

'I've got an idea. Wait here, Charlie.'

She watched as he ran across the gravel to the hot-dog van. She saw him open the back door and climb inside, emerging only a few seconds later carrying a metal ladder.

'Is that going to be long enough?' Charlotte asked when he returned.

'It's extendable,' he said. 'It'll just about reach the window.'

Dad watched anxiously as they positioned the ladder against the wall. Once again he looked nervous. Was it any wonder? thought Charlotte.

'Come on, Dad. We're waiting,' Harry called.

They both stood at the bottom, holding the ladder steady and looking up at the window. Dad hesitated for a moment before raising his hand to let them know he was ready. Then he turned and climbed backwards out of the window and felt for the top rung with his left foot. Carefully, he felt for the next. He was on his way.

While Dad climbed slowly down, Charlotte filled Harry in on what she had seen in Sikorsky's study.

'So something big is happening tonight, eh?' he said.

'It sounds like it, bro. We've got to contact the police. That's our only hope.'

'Right,' said Harry. 'We'll ring them and tell them what we know. There's a phone in Sikorsky's office. I saw it.'

'It's no good,' said Charlotte.

'What do you mean?'

'The phone. It got smashed. Sicko sat on it by mistake and it fell apart.'

Harry puffed out his cheeks and sighed. 'Then if we can't phone the police, we'll have to think of something else.'

'We need to get to the nearest house,' said Charlotte. 'We'll phone from there.'

By this time, Dad was no more than halfway down the ladder. 'Hurry up, Dad!' Harry called. 'We need to get away.' But they could tell he was still not fully recovered from his beating. He was unsteady and had to take his time. It was lucky that the light was fading and there was less chance that they would be spotted by Sikorsky's men.

Then, suddenly, they felt the ladder shudder in their hands. They looked up and saw Dad gripping onto the rung and shaking. There was something wrong. He was leaning heavily to one side.

'Keep moving, Dad,' Charlotte called. 'You're nearly down.'

They talked to him, encouraging him to continue his climb, but it was no use. He wouldn't move. He couldn't move. He hung on as if his feet were welded to the spot.

Then the ladder began to tip. In an attempt to keep it upright, the twins pushed with all their strength. But, no matter how they tried to stop it falling, they could not. Dad's weight was too much for them and the ladder toppled, swinging to the right with Dad hanging on. In spite of all their efforts, he finally crashed to the ground.

32
The Old Chapel

A large bush growing against the wall broke Dad's fall. He was badly shaken but, apart from bruises where the ladder fell on top of him, there were no serious injuries.

'I don't know what happened,' he said. 'I felt so dizzy up there, I couldn't move.'

Harry and Charlotte each took hold of one of his arms and helped him to his feet.

'No probs,' said Harry, once he was upright again. 'You're down on the ground now. We can get away.'

But Dad looked worried. 'Did anyone hear the noise, do you think?'

'Don't let's wait to find out,' said Charlotte. 'We're going back to the dormitory until you feel OK, Dad.'

The monastery was deserted, of course. The men were out searching the grounds and Sikorsky and Edina were nowhere to be seen. It took only a few minutes to reach the room where the monks slept.

As they opened the door, they saw Michael talking with the other brothers. Relief flooded over his face when he saw them and he spread his arms wide in welcome.

'My prayers have been answered!' he said, hugging the children to him before reaching out his hands to Dad. 'And this must be your father. It is especially good to meet you. Please sit. Heaven be praised you are safe.'

Dad was grateful of the chance to rest and he sank onto one of the beds. Exhausted by his climb, he lay back and closed his eyes.

Brother Michael turned to the children. 'We were so worried when you left the dormitory earlier,' he said. 'We wanted to help.'

'Sorry. We didn't dare wait,' Charlotte explained. 'We had to find Dad.'

'But we need your help now,' Harry said. 'Dad has to have somewhere to hide.'

After some discussion, the brothers agreed where he should go and what they would do to hide him.

'You *will* look after him, won't you?' Charlotte said. 'We can't stay. We have to get out of here and get help.'

Brother Michael nodded. 'Of course we'll take care of him,' he said. 'But I must warn you – it is almost impossible to leave the monastery. We have tried several times. You will be in danger, my children. These men are violent.'

'We know,' said Charlotte. 'But luckily they're quite stupid, too.'

Brother Michael smiled. 'Then go with our blessing. And pray that all goes well. We have tried several times to free our dear Father Abbot and failed.' He sighed a deep sigh and shook his head. 'Perhaps you will succeed where we have failed. We will help you all we can.'

'I suppose there are lots of hiding places in an old building like this,' said Harry.

'Indeed and we have one which will be perfect for your father.' Brother Michael glanced at his watch. 'Now it is time for Vespers.'

At this point, one of the brothers hurried out of the room.

'Brother Patrick has gone to ring the bell,' Brother Michael explained. 'We have evening prayers at this time every day. We go to the chapel which is a little way from the main building. Ivan Sikorsky took over our own chapel and forced us to use the old one.'

'So what's your plan?' asked Harry.

'First, your father must put on a habit. With the good Lord's help, no one will notice there are more of us going to Vespers tonight.'

Brother Michael turned and gently shook Dad awake while one of the others fetched a woollen habit and helped him to put it on.

'Sorry we can't go with you, Dad,' said Charlotte, sitting on the bed and taking his hand. 'There are things we have to do. We're going to get help.'

Dad looked up, half-asleep, his brow furrowed with concern. 'No, Charlotte. I can't let you go.'

'You're not well, Dad,' she said and put her arms round his shoulders. 'You must rest.'

'We just want you to hide for a few hours,' said Harry. 'We're going to get out of here and contact the police. Tell them about the reliquary and Sikorsky's criminal activities. All that stuff.'

Dad stood up slowly. He reached out and hugged them close. 'I am afraid for you both but I'm very proud of you. I only wish I could do something to help.'

As he spoke, a bell sounded from the chapel – a steady insistent ringing.

Brother Michael stepped forward. 'Bless you, my children,' he said. 'We will keep our part of the bargain.' He reached a small torch from the shelf and pressed it into Charlotte's hand. 'You may have need of this.'

'I don't suppose you've got a camera, have you?' asked Harry.

Charlotte stared at her brother. 'Harry?'

He winked. 'Good idea, eh? Evidence, my dear Watson!'

Brother Michael smiled. 'I understand,' he said. 'Yes, I have one over here. I've had it a long time but it still works.' Out of the top drawer of a wooden chest, he pulled a camera in a brown leather case. It looked rather old-fashioned, Harry thought, and was probably ten or even twenty years old. It was larger than the digital camera he had had for Christmas and much heavier. Still, if it worked, it could come in useful.

'Thanks,' said Harry and slung the strap across his chest.

Meanwhile, the other monks had picked up cushions and blankets; some food, too, and a bottle of water. Before the bell had stopped ringing, they had lined up in the corridor, their booty stuffed under their habits.

Brother Michael took hold of Dad – now dressed as a monk – and led him by the arm to the door. They walked in procession down the corridor and when they reached a door at the back of the building, Brother Michael turned to the twins. 'Your father will be safe with us,' he said. Then he walked on.

'Take care,' Dad called over his shoulder. 'Come back safe.'

The twins watched as the monks processed in silence, their hoods pulled over their heads, crossing the rough ground between the monastery and the old chapel. Brother Patrick had lit candles, which added a gentle glow to the distant building, and soon after the monks had disappeared inside, Harry and Charlotte heard the sound of the first hymn.

Dad was safe, for a while at least.

33
Electric Shock

Charlotte and Harry, standing in the shadow of the doorway, became aware of the sounds of men searching the grounds. Then voices inside the monastery. They had got out just in time.

'Tell me about that email on Sikorsky's laptop,' said Harry. 'What exactly did it say?'

Charlotte pulled the folded map out of her pocket. 'He's meeting someone at a place called Morgan's Point at half past eight.'

'But why's he going there?'

'Something illegal, you can bet,' she said. 'It mentioned Rotterdam in the email.'

They spread the map on the ground and shone the torch. Harry leaned close.

'We did Rotterdam in geography,' he said. 'It's a centre for diamonds, I think. But I'm not much good at geography.'

Charlotte pointed at the map. 'This is the area around Edinburgh. He's marked the monastery and, look, there's the nearest village.' She frowned and shook her head. 'It's miles away, Harry. We'll never get there before half past eight. Sikorsky will be finished at Morgan's Point before we've made the phone call – and he'll be away.'

'But he'll come back here, Charlie, and the police will still be able to arrest him.'

'And what if he doesn't come back? He might abandon the monastery. Things are getting difficult for him, aren't they? We know about the diamonds and that must make him very nervous. He'll be wondering who else knows. My bet is he'll do a runner and the police won't be able to find him.'

'We can't let that happen,' said Harry. 'We've no option but to go to Morgan's Point and find out what's going on. Take photos to show the police.'

'Agreed,' said Charlotte. 'Dad would want us to do that. He wouldn't want Sikorsky to get away.' She folded the map away and stuffed it in her pocket. 'Do you think we can walk there before half past eight?'

'Probably not,' said Harry. 'But I've got a great idea. Look over there.' He nodded in the direction of an old shed by the perimeter fence. It was long and low with a corrugated roof and, like most things connected with the monastery, it was in need of repair. But most importantly, it was stacked with bikes.

'If we ride,' said Harry, 'we'll get to Morgan's Point in plenty of time. Come on, sis. Let's go grab a bike while there's nobody around to see us.'

'What about the fence? How do we get over the fence?'

He shrugged. 'First we throw the bikes over and then we climb over. It's not all that high – a metre and a half at the most. You can climb that, can't you?'

'Can a crocodile swim?' she said.

They ran over to the shed and found eight bikes propped up in the stands. They were not modern bikes. No gears. No lightweight frames. They were old and hadn't been used for some time. As they checked them out, they discovered that three had flat tyres and two were so rusted that they were in imminent danger of crumbling away. It was likely that the brothers hadn't been cycling for some time. In the end, they found two which looked in reasonably good shape.

'I'll take this one,' said Harry, picking out a heavy black one, and he began pushing it towards the fence.

Charlotte took the other one from the stand and followed. But as they neared the perimeter, she suddenly said, 'Harry! Don't touch the fence. Stop!'

Harry spun round. 'What's got your knickers in a twist, Charlie?'

Charlotte was pointing to porcelain pots fixed on the metal posts. 'Look over there,' she said. 'Insulators.'

'What are insulators?' Harry said.

'We did them in science last term. Have you forgotten? Just think about it. Why would there be insulators on a fence?'

'Is this *Mastermind* or what?' Harry moaned. 'Science is not one of my best subjects, you know.'

Charlotte sighed. 'The fence must be *electrified*, of course. And from the size of the insulators, I'd guess there's a few hundred volts running through it.'

'No!' said Harry. 'That's rubbish.'

'I'll prove it,' said Charlotte. She fetched an old metal dustbin from the bike shed, dropped it onto its side and pushed it towards the fence so that it rolled over the grass. When it struck the wires, there was a sudden explosion of white sparks shooting over the fence and up into the evening sky like a massive firework display.

Harry stood there, his eyes wide with shock.

'W . . . we could have been killed,' he said.

'Right,' said Charlotte. 'Come on, Einstein. We'll have to come up with another way of getting out.'

34
Climb to Success

Harry ran on to check out the fence, leaving Charlotte holding the bikes. He needed to see if he could find a gap or a break where they might be able to squeeze through. All the time he was conscious that Sikorsky's men might not be far away. But he heard nothing. Maybe they had gone indoors, he thought. Maybe they had already left for Morgan's Point.

He inspected the fence until he came to the field where the horses were kept. For a second he wondered if they could ride the horses over to Morgan's Point. That would be cool. But could they jump over the electric fence? No. Of course they couldn't. Impossible.

It was as he walked on that he noticed the tree. It was next to a hay barn on the edge of the field – a solitary rowan tree, old and sturdy and, best of all, it overhung the fence.

'Yes!' said Harry, punching the air with his fist and turning to run back to Charlotte. 'There's a tree,' he panted. 'We can climb up it and drop over the other side without touching the fence. Come on. We're wasting time here.'

They hurried across the grass, pushing the bikes right up to the rowan.

'I'm going first,' said Charlotte.

Harry shook his head. 'Toss you for it.'

He pulled a coin from his pocket and spun it in the air, slapping it on the back of his hand. Charlotte won.

She was up the tree in no time. Harry lifted one of the bikes and passed it to her while she held onto the main trunk with one hand.

'Got it,' she called down. Then she flung the bike over the fence, clearing it easily.

'OK. Pass the next one,' she said and reached down to take it from Harry. This bike was older than the first with a heavy metal frame and took time to lift. She gripped it tight and tried to pull it up.

Harry was impatient. 'Go on, sis. Get on with it,' he called.

Charlotte took a deep breath and gritted her teeth as she swung her arm wide. Too wide. A pain shot through her shoulder as she released the bike. But the throw, no matter how hard she had tried, lacked power and she knew the bike would fall short. As she watched it rise up towards the fence and begin to drop again, her heart seemed to stop. She closed her eyes. She waited. Then she heard the crash of metal hitting the ground. Had the bike made it? She opened her eyes and, to her delight, she saw the bike on the other side of the fence.

'Good throw!' Harry called up. 'Now wriggle along the branch and drop over. Go on. It's easy.'

Charlotte sat on the branch that overhung the fence. 'All very well for you to say,' she whinged.

Her shoulder was still throbbing and she didn't dare jump. She knew that the branch she was perched across was stout and strong near to the main trunk but further away it grew thinner. No matter what Harry said, she knew that if she shuffled too far along it might not take her weight. But she forced herself to try. Bit by bit, she moved along – no more than a few centimetres at a time – until she was directly over the fence. All the time she kept her knees bent, making sure that her legs stayed well clear of the metal wire.

'Jump now!' Harry called.

Charlotte hung on, her stomach churning. She was frightened. She could break a leg or, worse, touch the fence on the way down and be shot through with a thousand volts of electricity.

'What's the matter?' Harry called again. 'Jump, Charlie! You'll be fine.'

She had two choices. She could go back and be trapped in the monastery. Or she could jump.

She chose the second.

She flung herself off the branch, flying over the fence, the ground racing towards her as she began to fall. Luckily, her landing was softened by thick tufts of heather. Even so, she lay on the ground for a while, winded and unable to believe that she was outside the perimeter. She was unhurt and she was safe.

'OK,' she called back to Harry who was already up the tree and settling on the branch. 'Your turn.' She struggled to her feet and waited for him to jump.

It was unfortunate that when Charlotte leaped over the fence, the branch had splintered in one spot, weakening it. Unknown to Harry, the crack was spreading along its length. He didn't see the danger until he was halfway, when he heard the branch snap and realized what was happening. Cold beads of sweat spread over his forehead. He looked down and saw the fence immediately below him. If the branch broke now, that would be the end. His heart was racing; frantically he wondered what he should do. He looked up. A smaller branch was above him and he reached for it.

By taking some of the weight off the other branch, he was able to move a little further forward.

But Charlotte could see what Harry couldn't. His action had not been enough to stop the lower branch from breaking. Any second now, it was going to snap.

'Jump! Now! Don't go further,' she called up to him.

Harry looked at her. 'Why?'

'Don't wait. JUMP! NOW! NOW!' she yelled.

As the branch gave its final crack, Harry launched himself into space, his arms spread-eagled, his knees bent, hoping to keep clear of the fence. Spinning in the air and with only millimetres to spare, he made it and landed with a thump on the heather next to his sister.

Now all they had to do was get to Morgan's Point.

35
A Bumpy Ride

Once they were outside the fence, Charlotte and Harry picked up the bikes and pushed them to the track which led away from the monastery and towards the main road. As drizzle began to fall, they climbed onto the saddles and began to ride along the rough and bumpy track. They wobbled a good deal, their wheels sometimes striking cobbles or dipping into potholes. But when they reached the main road, things were easier.

'This is the road I saw on the map,' said Charlotte as they picked up speed on the tarmac. 'We'll follow it for about two miles and then there should be a path off to the left that runs down to Morgan's Point.'

'Fine,' said Harry. 'If we stick to that route, we should be there in time.'

They agreed that they should try to hide from passing traffic. Any minute, Sikorsky could be heading this way. So whenever they heard the sound of a car or saw headlights, they jumped off their bikes and crouched at the side of the road to avoid being seen.

Harry was fed up. 'This is stupid. The heather's soaking wet.'

'If Sicko sees us, we're finished,' said Charlotte.

But Harry shook his head. 'Not likely. It's pretty dark. Even if he sees us, he won't *know* it's us.'

Half a mile further on, they heard another car some distance behind them. 'Hide,' said Charlotte but Harry refused. Then she grabbed his sleeve and pulled him into the undergrowth just before the car whizzed past. As they peered through the heather, they saw that the car was a black Land Rover Discovery.

'It's him!' said Charlotte. 'It was Sikorsky. I saw him and he had some of his cronies with him.'

Harry looked at his watch. 'They'll be there well before eight thirty. He must be nervous about being late.'

Confident now that the Russian was ahead of them, they didn't worry about the passing traffic. So when another car came in their direction, they just kept riding and didn't bother to look round. If they had, they would have seen Edina's Jaguar XJR bearing down on them, the beam of the headlights picking them out like a pair of rabbits. At the wheel, with her lips pressed tightly together, Edina Ross had no plans to overtake. She was aiming the car directly at the twins.

Almost too late, they realized what was happening. They flung themselves to the side just in time to avoid being turned into a nasty mess on the road.

'It was her!' said Charlotte, as the car flashed by. 'She nearly killed us.'

Harry struggled to sit up. 'Lucky escape. At least, she's gone now.'

'Don't count on it, bro. Just watch. She'll be back.'

Charlotte was right. Further along the road, the Jaguar screeched to a halt, skidding on the wet surface, then turned round and roared back in their direction.

'Run!' yelled Harry but Charlotte was already on her feet.

They abandoned the bikes and raced away into the darkness of the hillside, putting distance between them and the road. But, as they ran, the headlights of the car swung across the heath land, picking them out against the darkening sky so that Edina Ross could see them clearly. She wrenched the steering wheel hard to the right and the Jaguar spun off the road, plunging into the heather, rumbling over the bumpy ground. The headlights rocked up and down as the car lurched over the rutted heath, the beams catching Harry and Charlotte as they ran ahead. Even though the car was slower now, it was still gaining on them. Edina Ross leaned forward in the driver's seat, gripping the steering wheel and gritting her teeth. She was determined to catch them. She would run them down and flatten them if it was the last thing she did.

But the Jaguar XJR was not designed for off-road driving. The axles were low to the ground and the car struck one hummock too many and crunched to a halt. Full stop. It was going nowhere.

Edina Ross roared with anger and thumped her hands on the steering wheel. She turned the keys to try and start the engine. She pumped the accelerator. But the car couldn't move. The two men who were in the back seat leaped out, ran round the back and tried to push it out of the boggy patch. But it was no good. The more Edina revved the engine, the more the wheels spun, spraying the men with black goo and sending the car deeper into the sticky ground.

By then, Harry and Charlotte were well away from the headlights and they realized that they were no longer being followed. Then they stopped, resting their hands on their knees, gasping to recover their breath.

As the wind whipped up it blew the drizzle away, parting the clouds to make way for the moon. Now they could see more easily.

'If we stay parallel to the road,' Charlotte panted, 'we'll be OK. We should reach the track that leads to Morgan's Point.'

Harry nodded and, once their pulse rate had dropped to normal, they began to run again, constantly glancing in the direction of the road and checking their distance from it so they were never in danger of getting lost.

It took them a little more than half an hour before they spotted the path that led to the meeting place.

'We made it,' said Harry. 'We're nearly there, Charlie.'

Morgan's Point was a steep rocky outcrop jutting into the Firth of Forth. Down below was a narrow inlet, wide enough for a small boat to be out of sight of any passing ships that were heading for the port of Leith. And if they were in any doubt that they had found the right spot, the presence of Sikorsky's Land Rover parked on the cliff edge proved that they had.

'He's signalling,' said Charlotte as the car's head-lights flashed on and off. 'He's signalling out to sea.'

They stayed some distance away until the flashing stopped and the lights of the four-by-four had gone out. They heard the clunk of the doors as they opened. Then they saw the shadowy figures of four men climb out of the Land Rover and disappear over the cliff edge.

Harry squeezed his eyes. 'We've got to get down closer so we can see what's going on and take photographs.'

'There might still be someone in the car,' said Charlotte. 'Let's check it out.'

They ran across the heather, knees bent and heads low, until they came close to the back of the four-by-four. Charlotte put her hands on the side of the car and worked her way round to the driver's door before daring to peek in the window.

'It's empty,' she said. 'They're all down on the beach. Come on.'

But Harry wanted to look inside.

'Why?'

'Just need to see if there's any evidence and stuff.' He opened all four doors and peered into the spacious interior. 'Nothing except a packet of mints,' he said, reaching out and picking it up.

'Leave it, Harry,' Charlotte hissed. 'Sicko will notice.'

Reluctantly, he put it back before shutting the door and walking to the rear of the car and looking inside. Behind the back row of seats, he discovered a small space with a folded blanket. 'I wonder what's under it?' he said, and dragged it out. But there were only a few tools and an old map. Nothing of interest.

By this time, Charlotte was getting cross. 'Stop messing about, Harry. Come on. Let's go.' And she walked away towards the cliff path. Her brother quickly folded the blanket, closed the doors and ran after her.

The moon slipped out from behind a cloud and lit up the path for a few seconds. They needed to go carefully. The path was steep and if they slipped on the rocky surface, they would send a cascade of stones hurtling down. Sikorsky would surely send his men to see what was going on.

Another cloud soon plunged them back into darkness and they had to progress by feeling the bumpy ground through their trainers, gripping onto tufts of grass and slithering forward bit by bit. But when they finally reached the bottom, they found a large boulder which was a perfect hiding place and near enough to see what was going on.

All they had to do was watch and wait.

36
Morgan's Point

It was scary. Ivan Sikorsky was standing no more than fifty metres away from the twins. When the moon lit up the bay, they could see him clearly. They sat still, listening as his voice carried above the lapping of the water over the shingle.

'Fifteen minutes and Klaus Jansen will be here,' he said, glancing at his watch. 'You are all prepared, are you not?'

Boyle, Butterworth and LOVE HATE were nearby and pacing up and down the beach, patting their holsters. Each one held a Glock semi-automatic pistol.

'Just let him try anything funny,' said LOVE HATE, 'and he'll be a goner. Don't worry, boss. That's what we're here for.'

Ivan Sikorsky walked over and sat on a rock close to the water's edge and looked out to sea. 'Tomorrow we leave the monastery,' he said. 'Things are not good. I move on.'

'It's that Brodie fella, isn't it?' said Boyle. 'Sure he's

a pain in the neck what with the box thingy and the diamonds and those pesky kids. Sure, he—'

Butterworth dug him in the ribs to shut him up.

'He has, as you say, been a pain,' said Sikorsky. 'But I shall give myself the satisfaction of finishing off Mr James Brodie when I return to the monastery tonight.'

The Russian looked at his watch again – a gold Rolex Oyster – bold and beautiful in his eyes, paid for by an earlier shipment of diamonds. 'Where is Edina Ross?' he snapped. 'She is late. Surely she has not forgotten the rendezvous.' He pushed himself off the rock and stood up. 'Where is that stupid woman?' he shouted, looking around him.

LOVE HATE shrugged.

Butterworth said, 'Dunno.'

But Boyle ran enthusiastically towards the path calling, 'I'll find her. I'll find her. Sure, she might be up there where we left the Land Rover. Just leave it to me.'

He was already on the steep path, his trainers slipping on the rocky ground, causing an avalanche of stones behind him.

Sikorsky sighed. 'Forget her. It is too late,' he shouted. 'Come back at once. You are no good to me with the broken leg.'

Boyle knew better than to ignore his boss's order. Halfway up the path he stopped and turned round. Thinking that sliding back would be the fastest option, he crouched and set off with his seat skidding over the rough pathway. At first he was in control but as he continued, he moved faster and faster and the pieces of rock, half-buried in the ground, tore at his jeans and scraped the skin off his backside.

'Oooow, me bum!' he howled as he hit the beach. But he received no sympathy.

'Stand there!' Sikorsky ordered. 'Watch the horizon.'

The twins, still hiding behind the rock, wondered when something would happen. For several minutes, no one spoke and the only sound was the wind and the waves washing onto the shingle. Time ticked by. Then, in the distance, they heard the hum of a boat's engine and they knew that Klaus Jansen was on his way. The consignment was about to arrive.

'YOU,' Sikorsky snapped at Butterworth. 'Stand next to me. He expects to see two people. The rest of you get behind the rocks. Any sign of trouble and you shoot.'

Boyle and LOVE HATE scrambled over the boulders on the far side and hid behind them, while

Sikorsky and Butterworth stood side by side at the water's edge.

As the noise of the engine grew louder, Jansen's boat suddenly sprang out of the darkness, gleaming white and stainless steel, leaving a trail of foam behind. It was a Princess V53 V class, a superb sports yacht with a powerful remote-controlled searchlight which lit up the inlet as it approached. Then, some distance away from the shore, the sound of the engine died. The lights went out.

'What's he playing at?' Butterworth grumbled. 'What's he stopping out there for? Doesn't he know we're over here?'

Sikorsky turned his head away. 'You fool,' he sneered. 'If he comes into the shallow waters that very expensive boat will be ruined. Don't you know anything?'

'Well, I'm not swimming out to meet him,' said Butterworth.

'He will use the inflatable,' Sikorsky snapped. 'Just watch and you might learn something.'

In the past few minutes, a stiff breeze had sprung up, clearing the clouds so that the moon flooded the bay with a light as clear as day. Harry and Charlotte were able to see Klaus Jansen standing on the deck.

'Look at his dry suit,' she whispered to her brother. 'Black. Very sexy.'

Harry elbowed his sister. Girls! What are they like? He could see that Jansen was about thirty, tall and athletic with short blond hair. But no matter how good he looked, he was still a crook.

Jansen raised his hand to acknowledge Sikorsky and then he bent forward to let the anchor slip into the water. A second man stepped into view at the stern as he dragged out a small inflatable boat and dropped it over the side. Straightaway, Jansen slid into it and started up the motor while the men on the shore watched.

When the inflatable was near enough, Sikorsky called, 'Good evening, Klaus. You are on time exactly to the minute.'

The boat drifted up onto the shingle. 'I am always on time,' the Dutchman called as he sprang out onto the shore. 'It is you are often late, I think.'

Behind the rock, Charlotte turned to Harry. 'You'd better give me the camera,' she said. 'I'll take a photo. He's about to hand over the goods.'

Harry struggled to his feet and pulled the strap of the camera case over his head. 'I'll do it,' he said.

'Not with your glasses cracked. We don't want to take any risks.'

The Dutchman was walking towards Sikorsky. He was carrying a black leather briefcase in one hand and, when he got close, he held out his other hand in a businesslike manner.

'*Goede avond,*' his said, grasping Sikorsky's right hand and shaking it briefly. Then he looked at Butterworth. 'Where is Miss Ross?'

The Russian coughed. 'She's been unavoidably detained,' he said. 'This is Mr Butterworth, her colleague.'

'I only deal with top people,' he said, dismissing Butterworth like an unwanted fly on a piece of meat. 'No matter. Tonight I have no time to talk. I must not stay longer than is necessary. You know the problems.'

'Very well,' Sikorsky replied. 'Let us do business. I see you have the goods for me.' And he extended his hand to take the briefcase.

But Jansen pulled away so that it was out of reach. 'I prefer to see the money first. No?'

Sikorsky turned and signalled to Butterworth, who bent down and picked up a briefcase which was black and rectangular and very like Jansen's. Then he passed it across to the Dutchman.

'You will open it, please,' Jansen said.

Sikorsky nodded. He pulled a small key from his pocket, turned it in the lock and lifted the lid.

Charlotte gasped. In the clear moonlight, she could see that the case was packed with bundles of money. This was the time to take a photo. She raised the camera to her eye and pressed the button.

Jansen looked at the case full of money and nodded. '*Dat is goed*,' he said, taking the case then handing his own to Sikorsky.

The Russian clicked open the catch and looked inside. As he stared at the contents, he let out a growl which grew into an angry roar.

'What is this?' he shouted. 'This was not the deal. It is only half of what we agreed.'

Klaus Jansen shrugged. 'It is unfortunate, my friend, but things are difficult. Customs men are hot on my trail at the moment. Diamonds from certain parts of Africa . . . You know it is becoming more and more difficult, *doe je niet*? The price will be the same.'

Sikorsky was enraged. 'You will regret this,' he shouted, raising his fist as if to strike the Dutchman. 'This is the last time we do business.'

Jansen seemed unconcerned and began to walk towards the inflatable. He tossed the case of money into the little boat and pushed it into the water. 'So be it, my friend,' he said, holding his hands outstretched.

'I warned you that things were bad. This is not a good time to be in the diamond business.'

Charlotte took more photographs as Sikorsky followed the Dutchman into the shallows. 'Stop! You do not go, Jansen,' he called but the young man had already climbed into the dinghy and started the motor. 'You do not make fool out of me.'

Klaus Jansen turned to give a mock salute as he steered the inflatable towards his yacht. But he was not fast enough. He was not halfway there when a bullet from Sikorsky's Glock found its mark. He screamed and clutched his shoulder, feeling the thick warm blood ooze from the wound and seep between his fingers. And before he could reach for his own gun, another bullet struck him in the back and he fell over the side, his eyes wide open and staring as he sank into the cold black water.

Sikorsky turned to face his men, the gun hanging in his right hand. 'YOU!' he called to Boyle. 'Get the case out of the boat. I must have the money.'

Boyle stared at the sea. It looked very, very cold. Probably freezing. He didn't want to go.

The Russian yelled, 'GET IT NOW!' and raised his arm, pointing the Glock directly at him. 'FETCH ME THE MONEY OR ELSE.'

There was no choice. Afraid of the gun, Boyle resigned himself to more discomfort. He waded into the icy water and felt his circulation seize up immediately. He stopped and looked over his shoulder, hoping Sikorsky would call him back.

CRACK!

A bullet winged past him so close to his ear that he felt the draught. But he realized that the bullet had not been fired by Sikorsky. It came from Jansen's boat.

'Oh, Mother o' Mercy!' Boyle cried, not knowing which way to go. He had a gun pointing at him from the shore and one coming from the sea.

'GO, YOU FOOL,' shouted Sikorsky and fired a shot above his head. Terrified, Boyle waded forward until he was able to grab the side of the inflatable and tried to reach for the case.

Then CRACK! A second shot from Jansen's boat. This time it found its target and struck Boyle's arm. Shocked by the pain of it, he fell forward, collapsing into the dinghy.

Immediately, the men on the shore opened fire, aiming at Jansen's partner on the deck of his boat.

Sikorsky yelled at Butterworth, 'Leave the shooting to me. Go and get the case!'

The petrified Butterworth waded out, keeping his

knees bent and his head low to protect himself from the continuous gunfire. Bullets were flying in both directions, whistling over his head as he waded to the dinghy.

Then they stopped. Finally. Thank goodness. Butterworth heard the engine start up and saw the boat turn away from the cove and head towards Rotterdam. No more shooting. He was safe.

When he reached the inflatable, he found that Boyle was lying half in and half out of the dinghy groaning, 'Me arm! Me arm!'

He reached out and lifted him out of the boat, wrapping his good arm round his neck.

'No worries, pal,' said Butterworth. 'You'll be as right as rain when I get you back on dry land.'

But Sikorsky, watching from the shore, was furious. 'THE CASE, YOU IDIOT!' he bellowed, waving his gun. 'GET THE CASE!'

Balancing Boyle in his left arm, Butterworth leaned forward and somehow managed to scoop the case out of the dinghy in his free hand. With a great effort, he staggered back through the water and handed the case to Sikorsky.

The Russian was finally satisfied. Now he had both the diamonds and the money.

The past fifteen minutes had been full of action and had flashed by for Charlotte and Harry. They had seen everything and had captured the whole event on camera. All they had to do now was to take the evidence to the police and their worries would be over.

37
Fully Loaded

A heavy cloud drifted over the moon, blotting out the light.

'Quick! Let's go,' said Charlotte. 'Head up the path before they do.'

They set off while the four men were left on the beach arguing. What went wrong? Who did what? Who didn't do as he was ordered?

'We'll get to the top and get the bikes,' said Charlotte when they were halfway up the path.

'No chance of that,' said Harry. 'They're on the hillside somewhere. We'll never find them.'

'Then we'll have to walk.'

'No. It'll take ages. We've got to get back before Sikorsky finds Dad.'

'But how?'

'It's a long shot,' said Harry, climbing up the last step and onto the cliff top. 'There's a space at the back of the Land Rover. Remember the blanket?'

'We'll be squashed like sardines in a can,' said

Charlotte. 'We won't have much air to breathe. *And* there's a good chance we'll be found!'

'Got any better ideas?'

'No.'

Once Charlotte agreed to go along with Harry's plan, they hurried over to the four-by-four and opened the back door. Harry pulled out a box of tools and tossed it under a clump of broom.

'That will give us a bit more space,' he said.

The Land Rover Discovery had three rows of seats and behind the third row was a small area for shopping bags. It was very small but, if they pushed their feet under the seats, they could just about squash in.

Charlotte climbed over the high lip into the cramped space and was about to cover herself with the blanket when they heard voices coming from the cliff path. Sikorsky was talking to LOVE HATE and they could hear Boyle making terrible noises. They were already heading back to the car.

Quickly, Harry climbed in, swung the door shut again and pulled the blanket over their heads so that they were completely covered. They lay there, holding their breath and waiting.

The men were getting nearer.

'For all your stupidity,' said Sikorsky, 'tonight has worked out splendidly.' He opened the front door and climbed into the driver's seat. 'Klaus Jansen was no match for me, you can be sure.'

LOVE HATE, saying nothing, sat next to him.

Then they heard, 'Oh, me arm, me arm!' as Boyle, climbed into the second row with Butterworth.

'Put these in the back,' Sikorsky ordered and the twins heard him pass something to Butterworth who only said, 'Right, boss.' Then he threw first one object and then a second onto the back row of seats. Harry and Charlotte guessed they were two cases. They were so near, they could almost touch them.

Before Sikorsky started the engine, he barked instructions at Butterworth. 'I will not have the blood dripping over the car. Remove your sweater and put it in on the wound.'

Butterworth, who was very cold and wet, pulled his jumper over his head and wrapped it round his mate's shoulder.

But Boyle screamed with the pain. 'Aaaaaaaaaaaaaaagh! Leave me alone, Kevin! Aaaaaaaaagh! Me arm!'

'Control yourself,' Sikorsky snapped as he turned the key in the ignition. 'It is a scratch. Nothing more.' And he began to reverse.

'It's terrible, I tell you,' Boyle moaned as they bumped down the track. 'Aaaaaaaaaaaaagh! Me arm!'

'Keep him quiet,' yelled Sikorsky. 'He gives me the headache.'

Butterworth slapped his hand over Boyle's mouth. 'I'll do me best, boss,' he said.

Once the noise was muffled, Sikorsky relaxed. 'A good night's work, huh? We have the money back.'

LOVE HATE snorted. 'We wouldn't want to leave it for the sea gulls, would we, boss?'

'I doubt that sea gulls would be interested in the briefcase,' he said. 'But someone might have found it. It was essential to get it back. So now we have the diamonds and the money. Very satisfying, eh?'

'That Dutch fella was a nasty double dealer, wasn't he?' said LOVE HATE. 'He got what he deserved.'

'Mmmmm mmmmm,' Boyle whined.

Sikorsky was triumphant. 'Indeed so. And when the body is washed up further down the coast,' he laughed, 'I shall be hundreds of miles away.'

The four-by-four had bumped over the rough ground – uncomfortable for the twins – but now it had reached the end of the track and had turned onto the smooth tarmac of the main road and picked up speed. But under the blanket, the temperature was

199

rising. Harry and Charlotte were sweating, crammed together like peas in a pod. They desperately hoped that the journey would soon be over and they would arrive before they were discovered.

Suddenly, they felt the Land Rover swerve to the opposite side of the road and stop. Sikorsky pressed the button to lower the window and leaned out. 'What are you doing here?' he shouted.

Then they heard the voice of Edina Ross, shrill and panicky. 'I had an accident,' she said. 'I had to abandon my car. We were walking back to get help.'

Sikorsky snorted. 'And what happened to these two? They look as if they have taken a bath in mud.'

'They tried to push my car out of the bog,' she explained. 'I'm afraid they got a little . . . er . . . splashed.'

'More than can be said for you, Edina. Your shoes may be ruined but you are otherwise immaculate, are you not?'

'I would be very glad of a lift,' she said, ignoring his rudeness. 'It's rather a long walk to the monastery.'

There was an awkward silence, then Sikorsky snapped, 'You two! Take off your trousers and your sweaters. Leave them on the grass – they're filthy.

I won't have you in my car while you wear them, huh?'

The two men stripped off until they were left shivering in their underpants.

'Get in,' barked Sikorsky.

The men climbed into the back seats, moving the briefcases out of the way and tossing them into the space behind. Crash! They fell heavily on Harry and Charlotte and it was all they could do to stop themselves yelling out loud.

Sikorsky instructed LOVE HATE to get out and sit in the second row with Boyle and Butterworth. He was not pleased. He slumped onto the seat next to Boyle, pushing against him to make room. This resulted in an ear-shattering yell from the injured Boyle and another rebuke from Sikorsky.

When Edina Ross began to climb into the front seat, the Russian yelled, 'No, no no! Take off the shoes! They are quite disgusting.'

'Oh, of course,' she said and bent down and slipped off her expensive, suede high heels. She was about to carry them into the four-by-four when Sikorsky shouted again. 'LEAVE THEM! I will not have the filthy things in my car.'

Remembering how much they had cost, she was reluctant to leave them. But if she wanted a ride, she had no choice. She finally tossed them onto the heather before climbing barefoot into the front seat.

'And how,' asked Sikorsky as the car moved off, 'did you get your car stuck in a bog?'

'It was those children,' she explained. 'I saw them riding bikes along this road.'

'This road?'

'Yes. I tried to follow them but they ran over the heather and I'm afraid my car got bogged down. We couldn't move it. We tried.'

'I can see that,' said Sikorsky, sounding rather pleased at her bad fortune. 'You should get yourself a decent car, Edina. That one of yours is no more than a tin can.'

Edina's sigh of exasperation was audible but she said nothing in reply. Sikorsky, however, was planning what to do next.

'So the children got out of the monastery grounds? I expect they were trying to reach a village to get help.'

'Yes, probably.'

'But they were heading the wrong way, no? There isn't a village for miles in that direction.'

'They abandoned their bikes on the hill,' she explained. 'We found them.'

'Good. That will slow them down. But even so, they might reach somewhere by morning.'

'Or somebody might give them a lift,' said Edina.

For a moment there was silence. Then Sikorsky spoke. 'I had planned to leave the monastery tomorrow,' he said, tapping his fingers on the steering wheel, 'but I have decided we should leave tonight. As soon as we get back, we pack everything and clear the workshop. We must not leave anything behind that might lead the police to us.'

'What about James Brodie?'

Harry and Charlotte strained their ears to catch every word.

'I originally planned to let him go once the operation in Scotland was finished,' he said. 'But I no longer feel so kind towards him.' The Russian paused for a moment before he said, 'Things are different now. He should be punished for having difficult children, no? As soon as I return, I think he will meet with an unfortunate accident.'

38
Bonfire Night

After an uncomfortable ride, Harry and Charlotte were relieved when the Land Rover Discovery turned off the main road and rumbled over the track that led to the monastery. Ivan Sikorsky reached for his remote control, pointed it at the gate and the car rolled through. He stopped in the parking area in front of the building and the twins heard footsteps running from the main door and men shouting 'Mr Sikorsky!'

The Russian climbed out of the four-by-four. 'What is this?' he asked. 'What is the fuss?'

The men were breathless. 'We found it,' they panted.

'What? Speak out.'

'We found the key to the bedroom.'

'Good. Good,' said Sikorsky, swinging his legs out of the car. 'I have plans for Mr Brodie.'

'No,' said one of the men. 'It's not good. He wasn't there. He'd got out through the window. It was wide open. There was a ladder.'

Sikorsky howled with anger. 'No! Catastrophe! Those children must have got him out. We go! We leave!' He raged as he issued instructions to his men. 'Fill the vans with the equipment from the work-shops. Take everything. We leave in half an hour.'

Harry and Charlotte felt the Land Rover shake as they all jumped out. It must have been an odd sight, they thought. Edina with no shoes. Butterworth in his vest. Boyle hobbling along, clutching his wound. And the others in their underpants.

Their voices faded as they hurried inside the monastery, giving the twins the perfect opportunity to climb out of the four-by-four. Not that it was easy. They had been folded up so tightly that their legs were cramped and stiff and it took time to stretch them out and get them back into working order.

'We've got to do two things,' said Harry when they had recovered. 'We have to get the police here as soon as possible and we've got to stop Sikorsky leaving.'

'How do we call the police, brainbox? There's no phone.'

'No. But I've had another genius idea.'

'Like what?'

'If there are horses, there's sure to be hay in the barn.'

'And?'

'We could set light to them. Someone in the village will see it for certain and dial 999.'

'Brilliant, bro!' said Charlotte and they gave a high-five before they set off running to the barn.

Harry was right. The barn was full of hay and it would burn quickly, lighting up the night sky. But there was a snag to their plan. The brothers had put their two beloved horses in the stables for the night – and the stables were next to the barn. So it would be too dangerous to set fire to the hay. The horses would be terrified and the stables would probably catch fire.

'We'll take the horses over to the far field,' Harry suggested.

'No, they'll make a noise,' Charlotte said. 'Somebody might come to see what's going on. No. I've got a better idea. If we move the bales over to the far side, we could set fire to them there.'

It was the answer to the problem. They went into the barn and began to move the bales. They heaved and pushed and kicked until there were ten of them well away from the stables.

'OK,' said Charlotte. 'You do the honours. I can't wait to see the flames. This is going to be better than bonfire night.'

But they had overlooked one thing. They had no matches.

'There must be matches somewhere,' said Charlotte.

'I know,' said Harry. 'Brother Patrick lit the candles in the chapel, right? So there must be matches. Let's go. We'll check that Dad's OK at the same time.'

They hurried round the back of the monastery which was heavily cast in deep shadows. The moon came out in fits and starts. Lighting up the night like a beacon one minute and the next, hiding behind a cloud so that darkness fell like a thick blanket over everything. They ran across the grass, constantly on the lookout for Sikorsky's men. They passed the door at the back of the building and, further along, stepped through the rough ground to the oldest part of the monastery. Without being spotted, they finally arrived at the chapel itself.

Vespers was over long ago and there was no candle-light now. The chapel was in total darkness. Slowly, they pushed open the great wooden door, afraid of making any noise. But, once they were inside and the door shut again, Harry called, 'Dad! It's us. We're coming.'

With the door shut, the chapel was dark as ink so that they had to feel their way down the aisle, holding onto the sides of the pews, towards the altar.

'Dad!' Harry repeated. 'Dad! Are you OK? Where are you?'

They heard a rustle from the far end. They stood still and listened. Then they heard it again.

'What is it?' whispered Charlotte.

'Don't know,' Harry whispered in reply.

Then someone spoke.

'I'm OK.'

It was Dad. Relief swept over the twins and they hurried down to the altar to join him.

'Sorry,' he said. 'I was asleep.' Of course he'd been asleep. He was still recovering from his beating.

'Dad,' said Charlotte, helping him to sit up. 'We're going to get the police and the fire brigade. They'll be here before you know it.'

Then they explained their plan to him.

'You two are amazing,' he said. 'I can't tell you how proud of you I am.'

'We're not that amazing,' said Harry. 'We haven't got any matches.'

'That's something I can help with,' Dad said and reached under the blanket. 'Brother Michael gave me these.' He struggled to stand up. 'I must help you. I'm coming, too.'

But it was obvious that he was still too weak.

'If the men come out,' said Charlotte, 'we might have to run and hide. You're just not well enough,

Dad. Not yet. Please wait here for a bit longer. Please.'

He sank down onto the floor again and held his head in his hands. 'You're right,' he said. Then he looked up again. 'But the hay will only burn for a short time. Have you thought of that? And what if the villagers don't see the fire? They could be in bed.'

The twins looked at each other and . . . *ching!* . . . a light went on in their brains. It was as if they had thought of the same idea at exactly the same time.

'Dad,' said Charlotte, 'do you think you could ring the chapel bell? That will wake people up. You can hear it for miles.'

Dad thought it was a great idea. 'I'll wait for five or six minutes,' he said. 'That should give you time to light the hay – then I'll pull on the bell rope. When they hear it, the villagers will know something's wrong.'

'And they'll realize there's a fire,' said Harry, 'because the blaze will light up the sky. It'll be like a mega bonfire.'

'Brilliant!' said Charlotte. 'Brilliant, brilliant, brilliant!' And she hugged Dad. 'We're going to get out of here after all. Come on, Harry. Let's go.'

39
Bell Ringing

They ran back to the field where they had left the hay. The earlier rain had stopped but now a wind had whipped up.

'Take some of the hay out of the bales, Harry,' said Charlotte. 'Loose hay will be easier to set alight.'

The small piles they made alongside the bales got caught up in the breeze and rolled away like tumbleweed. So they snapped branches off nearby trees to weight them down.

Harry pulled the box out of his pocket and struck one match and then another but gusts of wind blew them out.

'Come and shelter the flame,' he said. 'We can't afford to waste any more matches. The box is nearly empty.'

Charlotte cupped her hands around the match so that when Harry struck the next one, it stayed alight.

'Good one, sis,' he said as he bent down to light the hay but before the flame made contact, it went out again.

Before Harry had taken the next match from the box, the sound of the bell erupted from the chapel. Dad was pulling on the rope in sharp, regular pulls. Two rings every second.

DONG DONG DONG DONG

The wind blew the sound of the bell across the hill and down to the village miles away, filling the night with alarm. People woke and sat up rubbing their eyes, wondering what could be wrong. They climbed out of their beds to look out of the windows. But there was no fire for them to see.

The bell kept ringing as Harry finally struck a match. This time it stayed alight long enough to light the first pile of hay. In seconds it burst into flames, leaping into the black sky and spreading from one bale to the next. Before long, all the bales were alight. Harry and Charlotte watched as flames and smoke reached higher and higher. They gazed, open-mouthed, amazed that they had done it at last.

The villagers were not the only ones to hear the bell, of course. Sikorsky and his men, busy packing up their equipment, heard it.

'Find who is ringing that bell!' Sikorsky shouted at Boyle and Butterworth. 'If those monks are playing tricks, they will regret it and so will their Father Abbot.'

Butterworth ran out towards the chapel while Boyle was well behind him, limping as fast as he could, clutching his injured shoulder. But when Butterworth tried to open the chapel door, he found that it was shut fast. Dad had somehow managed to push a heavy oak pew behind it in an attempt to keep Sikorsky's men out.

When Boyle arrived at the chapel he said, 'I think there's somebody in there, Kevin.'

'Oh,' said Butterworth. 'Who would have thought it, eh? What with the bell ringing and that.' Then he whopped Boyle across the head. 'Help me push it open, you daft oaf. They've put something behind it.'

'Me left arm hurts,' Boyle complained.

'Your right arm will hurt in a minute,' said Butterworth with a sigh of exasperation. 'Now come on.'

The two men put their backs against the door and pushed while the bell continued to ring DONG DONG DONG DONG. Eventually, little by little, it opened until there was a gap big enough for them to squeeze through.

'Where's the bell?' Butterworth said as they felt their way between the lines of pews.

'How would I know?' said Boyle. 'It's as dark as pitch in here. Which way shall we go?'

'We should have brought the torches,' Butterworth said peevishly.

'Shall I go back for them?'

'No. We'll be able to find the bell in a place as small as this. Use your ears, man. Where's the noise coming from?'

'On the roof,' said Boyle.

'I know the bell's on the roof, idiot! But there's somebody pulling on a rope. And the rope isn't on the roof, is it?'

James Brodie was standing in the small bell tower just to the side of the chapel. He desperately needed to take a rest but he kept pulling, knowing it would not be long before the men found him.

But one thing stopped Boyle and Butterworth in their tracks. Now that the hay was well alight, the red glow of the flames spread through the open doors of the chapel so that the walls turned a gentle pink.

'I don't believe it!' Butterworth cried. 'The field's on fire. Dermot, you find this bloke who's ringing the bell and stop him. I'm going to see what's happening out there.'

Abandoning his search of the chapel, Butterworth ran out and raced towards the field just as the brothers poured out of the back door. They had heard the bell. Now they could see the fire, too.

'What's going on?' asked Brother Michael, running beside Butterworth.

'You should know!' Butterworth snapped. 'I bet it's you lot that did it!'

'And why would we set fire to a field? The animals will be terrified,' Brother Michael replied.

'Never mind the animals,' shouted Butterworth. 'Just help me douse the fire. We don't want the fire brigade called out, do we?'

'Ah, yes,' said Brother Michael. 'The fire brigade.' And he suddenly understood what was happening. The twins had lit the bales for a very good reason. The last thing he wanted to do was to put it out. He stood still, gazing at the flames and smiling.

Butterworth, however, did his best to put out the fire. He tore off his vest and began flapping it at the flames like a wild thing. But the vest, which was a thin tattered garment, soon caught fire and, for lack of anything else, he ripped off his trousers and used those.

'Why don't you come and help!' he yelled at the monks as he jumped about – first one way and then another – beating pointlessly at the flames, trying to stop the fire spreading.

'We must go and move the animals,' Brother Michael called above the noise of Butterworth's swearing. 'Brother Patrick, you take some of the brothers and move the pigs. The rest of us will see to the horses.'

Butterworth went totally berserk. 'What are you thinking of?' he yelled hysterically, whacking at the flames with his trousers. 'It doesn't take all you lot to move a few animals. Come back!'

But the brothers were well on their way, hurrying across the field.

Then the bell stopped ringing and in the silence that followed, Butterworth shouted again, hoping that someone inside the monastery would hear.

'Fire! Come quick! Heeeeeeeeeeeeeeeeelp!' he screamed again and again.

But nobody seemed to hear him. None of Sikorsky's men came to help him. Or maybe they were more interested in getting away. Time was running out.

In spite of Butterworth's athletic jumps and dramatic attempts to control the fire, the flames spread quickly and eventually he stood back, defeated and exhausted, his hair singed, his skin blackened by the smoke.

Meanwhile, Harry and Charlotte were racing back to the chapel. Dad had stopped ringing the bell and they had to find out if he was OK. When they saw that the chapel door was wide open, they knew he was in trouble. They ran inside. Noises. Grunts. Shouts. What was going on? They hared down the aisle and found Dad on the floor. He was wrestling with Boyle; they were rolling over and over, fighting like schoolboys. Boyle was shouting, 'Ow! Me arm!' Then, 'Ow! Me foot!'

The twins were desperate to help Dad. But how could they stop this bull of a man? He may have injuries but he was still much stronger than Dad. Charlotte looked around for some kind of weapon and found a candlestick up on the altar.

'This'll have to do,' she muttered and held it up ready to strike Boyle.

'No,' said Harry. 'You might hit Dad.'

Harry was right. As the two men rolled, it was difficult to see which was Boyle and which was Dad. But in the light through the open door, Charlotte found it easiest to focus on their shoes. Dad's were brown leather and Boyle's were dirty trainers. For one second, she had a clear view of Boyle's feet. She grabbed the opportunity and swung the candlestick. Target! It struck his ankle bone.

'Aaaaaaaaaaaagh!' Boyle let out an excruciating

scream and let go his grip on Dad, curling up on the floor, clinging to his foot and howling like a baby.

The twins helped Dad to his feet. 'Thanks,' he said. 'Now you sit on him, will you, and I'll tie his hands.'

Dad removed the rope from the monk's habit he was wearing while Charlotte sat on Boyle's legs and Harry sat on his stomach. Dad pulled Boyle's arms together and wrapped the thick rope around them.

'Watch me shoulder!' yelled Boyle. 'And me foot . . . and me ankle!'

Once his hands were tied, he lay still on the floor, groaning, and Dad sank onto the nearest pew, completely exhausted.

'Give me a minute,' he panted. 'I'll be fine. And thanks for getting him off me. He fights like a tiger.'

The twins sat beside Dad, ignoring Boyle's curses. As they waited in the darkness of the chapel, they heard a noise from the far side of the monastery. There was no doubting what it was. It was the sound of a car engine starting up.

Harry and Charlotte leaped to their feet.

'That's the Land Rover,' said Harry. 'Sicko's leaving already. We're going to lose him if we don't do something. We've got to stop him.'

Dad had no energy to protest as they left him and

ran out of the chapel. They raced round the side of the monastery, past the flaming hay and on to the car park.

The Land Rover was already moving, heading down the drive.

Too late! There was no way Harry and Charlotte could catch up with it. And what would be the point? How could they stop Sikorsky getting away now?

40
Heaven for Pigs

The twins stood watching the Land Rover roll down the drive and knew they had lost their battle to hand Sikorsky to the police. They had started the fire too late. The Russian would be gone by the time the fire brigade and the police arrived. What was the point of everything they had done? Sikorsky would be on a plane in an hour or so. He would be miles away and in another country.

But, before the Land Rover had reached the gate, Charlotte saw something in the red light of the fire.

'Look!' she said, pointing to the field. 'There's something moving over there. I think it's Brother Patrick.'

Harry peered into the distance. 'What's he doing?'

The monk was hurrying towards the gate, followed by twenty large Gloucester Old Spots. These were a rare breed of pig with black spots which made them look like the porky equivalent of Dalmatians. Nineteen of them were sows and one, the largest of them all, was a boar. He was named Samson – a fierce-looking animal whose tusks had become incredibly long with age.

The twins knew that the monks were very fond of the pigs. They had lovingly cared for them for years. But why were they following Brother Michael like the Pied Piper? The reason was simple. In the crook of his left arm, he was holding a sack of pig food. A kind of Heaven for Pigs.

Charlotte grinned. 'Maybe Sicko won't get away, after all.'

'How do you mean?'

'Just watch. I think I can guess what he's going to do.'

The monk and the pigs reached the gate as the Land Rover approached and picked them out in the glare of its headlights. Harry and Charlotte whooped in delight as they saw Brother Michael tip the contents of the sack onto the ground in front of the gate. The animals rushed forward, jostling with each other and grunting loudly, fighting to get at their unexpected feast.

Now there was a heap of food and twenty hungry pigs between the Land Rover and the gate.

Sikorsky leaned out of the window and screamed, 'What are you doing? Get those animals out of the way.'

But he was shouting into thin air. Brother Michael had mysteriously disappeared.

The Russian jumped out of the car in a black rage, bawling at the pigs. But none of them took any notice except for Samson. He slowly turned his head to see who was making such a fuss and interrupting his delicious meal. When he saw the tubby Russian jumping up and down and waving his arms in the air, he became very annoyed. He fixed him with his piggy stare, lowered his head and began to walk towards him.

'Go away!' Sikorsky shouted, but Samson did no such thing. Instead, he picked up speed and the Russian, terrified by the sight of those fierce tusks, went leaping back into the Land Rover, slamming the door shut. He was so enraged by the situation that he thumped his hand on the horn, hoping that the noise would frighten the pigs away from the gateway.

But it didn't.

'Use your gun,' said Edina Ross. 'Shoot them.'

Sikorsky turned to her with a look of disgust on his face. 'How will that help, you stupid woman? Twenty dead pigs in the gateway would be even worse.'

Unless he could think of something fast, his escape was doomed.

41
No Way Ahead

'So far, so good,' said Harry.

Then, by the light of the full moon, Charlotte spotted Butterworth running round the side of the monastery. 'Look,' she said. 'He's in his underpants and he's black with smoke! He must have been trying to beat out the flames.'

Harry laughed. 'I bet he heard the Land Rover start up and he knew Sikorsky was leaving without him.'

They watched Butterworth run over to the hot-dog van and arrive at the same time as Boyle.

'His hands are still tied,' said Harry. 'Don't know how he managed to get out of the chapel.'

Butterworth was pointing to the rope around Boyle's wrists. 'You great buffoon,' he yelled. 'How did that happen? James Brodie was a sick man. A weakling.'

'I was overpowered,' Boyle lied. 'Sure, there were fifteen of them. Maybe more.'

There was no time for arguments. Butterworth untied the rope and they both jumped into the van and set off down the drive until they came to a full stop behind the Land Rover.

'What's going on?' said Butterworth, sticking his head out of the window. 'Why are they stopped?'

Boyle climbed out of the van. 'It's just a few pigs,' he said. 'Come on. We'll soon have them out of the way.'

He limped towards the Land Rover.

'Don't you worry, Mr S,' he called as he passed the open window of the Discovery. 'I'm used to pigs, so I am.' He began to wave his arms at the animals, not noticing that Samson was irritated at having his unexpected feast disturbed yet again.

Butterworth, following behind, pointed to the pig food on the drive. 'No wonder they won't move,' he said. 'Pick it up, Dermot. Go on. They'll move then.'

Boyle looked suspiciously at his partner.

'Oh aye. And why don't you do it, eh? Me arm's bad. And me foot. Why me?'

'You're shorter than me,' Butterworth replied. 'You're nearer to the ground. Anyway, I'm the boss.'

Unwillingly, Boyle gave in and pushed his way through the pigs to the heap of food. He bent down to pick up a handful and threw it to the side of the drive. Two of the sows followed the food, the rest stayed put. Boyle bent down again to take another handful but this was the final straw for Samson. With Boyle's backside in full view, the pig was unable to resist. He lowered his head, charged towards him and sank his tusks into the soft flesh of his buttocks.

Boyle let out a howl of agony. 'Aaaaaaaaaaaaaaagh!' and raced back to the van, clutching his bottom, with Samson in pursuit.

Sikorsky was furious. He leaned out of the car window and shouted to Butterworth. 'That man is useless. You go and move the food. Quickly!'

Butterworth shook his head. 'Too dangerous,' he said. 'I'm getting out of the way.'

But as he reached the van and grasped the door handle, Sikorsky pointed his gun and fired it over his head. The bullet pinged off the hot dog on the roof and sent bits of brown plastic scattering onto the drive. Butterworth froze.

'DO IT!' Sikorsky shouted.

Butterworth was too terrified to move, so the Russian fired again. This time punching a large hole through the middle of the sausage.

'NOW!' he yelled.

Shaking from head to foot, Butterworth looked at

the pigs and he looked at the gun. Neither was a great choice. But the gun was the worst.

'Right! Right away, Mr Sikorsky,' he called and he moved towards the pigs and cautiously pushed his way into the middle of them.

All the problems with the pigs had given the twins valuable minutes in which to do something. They were able to sneak round the back of the Land Rover without being seen. They crouched down, Harry on the left and Charlotte on the right, and began to twist the valves on the tyres and press them to release the air. When the rear tyres were as flat as pancakes, they moved to the back of the hot-dog van and let the air out of those tyres, too.

Job well done.

Butterworth finally succeeded in moving the pigs off the drive by scattering the food onto the field. Sikorsky could hardly contain his exasperation with the delay as the last pigs wandered away. Only then was he able to click his remote to open the gate.

'At last,' he said as it swung open. The Land Rover engine roared and, just as the Russian felt his escape was imminent, he heard a noise in the distance. 'What is that?' he asked as it grew louder.

'A fire engine,' Edina Ross replied. 'It's on its way to put out the fire.'

'We get out just in time, I think,' Sikorsky said as he slipped into first gear. But when the car began to move, it would only inch forward on its flattened tyres, very very slowly.

'WHAT NOW?' he ranted, pressing his foot hard on the accelerator.

'You must get it moving,' snapped Edina Ross, 'or the fire brigade will be here.'

Sikorsky turned, red faced, and glowered at her. 'Don't you think I know that? I think this whole business is your fault, you crazy woman. If you hadn't made the mistake with that reliquary, none of this would have happened.'

There was a tapping noise on his window. It was Butterworth.

'What is it?' Sikorsky barked.

'It's your tyres, sir. Somebody's let the air out. They're flat as a plate of soup.' He smiled apologetically as if it was his fault.

Sikorsky ground his teeth and thumped his hand on the steering wheel again. 'No, no, no!' he shouted, 'What is going on here?' Then, without a word to anyone, he reached into his jacket, pulled out his mobile phone and dialled.

The twins saw all this happen and watched with satisfaction as the fire engine finally turned off the main road and headed up the track to the gate. In less than a minute, it was there. It stopped and the crew commander leaped down from the cab and walked over to Ivan Sikorsky.

'You'll have to move your car, sir,' he called. 'We need to get in. Where exactly is the fire?'

'It is round the back,' said Sikorsky, leaning out of the window. 'But I can't move my car. The tyres have been let down.'

The fireman raised his eyebrows in surprise. 'And who would do that, sir?'

Before Sikorsky could answer, Harry and Charlotte appeared round the front of the Land Rover.

'We did it,' said Harry. 'We had to stop them getting away.'

Sikorsky rolled his eyes in disbelief. 'You must arrest them at once,' he screamed. 'Get this boy out of my way.'

The crew commander leaned forward and put his hand on Harry's shoulder. 'Did you start the fire, son?'

'Yes. We had to attract your attention.'

'We were hoping the police would come, too,' said Charlotte. 'Where are they?'

The fireman wasn't interested. 'I suppose you know that starting a fire is a criminal offence,' he said. 'You two could be in serious trouble.'

They didn't answer. They were distracted by the sight of Boyle and Butterworth running across the field. They were about to make their escape.

'Stop them!' Charlotte yelled, pointing at the men. 'They're part of the gang. Don't let them get away.'

42
Our Very Own Cop Show

'Come on, Dermot,' said Butterworth. 'We don't want to get caught by the old Bill.'

'What about me arm?' Boyle asked.

'You don't need your arm to run, you fool,' Butterworth replied.

'What about me foot and me leg?'

Butterworth ignored him.

'And me backside's sore, too, Kevin.'

Furious, Butterworth grabbed Boyle by his sweater and pulled him close until they were nose to nose. 'I don't care about your arm or your foot or your leg or your backside,' he growled through gritted teeth. 'JUST MOVE!'

As they ran away from the van, Butterworth pointed to the far corner of the field and their means of escape. 'See, Dermot! Horses!'

'I can see them,' Boyle replied, trying to keep up. 'Very nice.'

'You can ride, can't you?'

'Since I was knee-high to a grasshopper.'

'Then we're saved,' said Butterworth. 'Head over the field. We're going to ride out away from this place.'

Boyle was holding onto his injured arm and limping badly since his confrontation with Samson. 'Not so fast,' he gasped. 'Me bottom's bad.'

'Ah, stop your narpin', will you?' said Butterworth. 'There isn't a part of you that's not in a state.'

In spite of everything, Boyle tried to follow. Ahead of them, were the ponies which had been led out of the stables and away from the flames. Two brothers were standing with them, holding their lead reins and talking to them in soft, comforting tones.

The ponies, called Bonnie and Rio, had been with the brothers for over three years, ever since they had been rescued from the knacker's yard on the outskirts of Glasgow. Bonnie was a shaggy black fell pony, thirteen hands high with a stubborn streak. Rio was a dark bay Welsh cob, two hands taller than Bonnie and inclined to go wild and kick his heels whenever the fancy took him.

'What about saddles?' Boyle asked. 'Do you think they have saddles?'

'Saddles?' snorted Butterworth. 'Just leap on their back, man. This isn't the Horse of the Year Show.'

The monks holding the ponies were alarmed to see the men heading their way and realized that they intended to snatch the animals and ride off. But they were determined not to let that happen. They did the only thing they could – they let go of the lead ropes and slapped the ponies on their rumps.

'Wow! Off you go, Bonnie!' they shouted. 'You too, Rio!' And the ponies galloped away, glad to be free.

Boyle jumped up and down. 'You stupid old men!' he shouted. 'What did you do that for?'

But Butterworth didn't waste time. 'Don't just stand there, you great idiot. Run after them.'

Catching them seemed impossible. But the truth was, Bonnie and Rio were glad to be out of the stable and soon slowed down to graze on the sweet long grass. Boyle and Butterworth were able to creep up behind them and, when they were close, they launched themselves onto the ponies' backs, surprising the animals so that they took off.

Butterworth did rather well riding bareback but Boyle found it difficult to swing his leg over Rio because of his injuries. He had to ride, flopping across the pony, hanging onto its mane with his good arm.

They were heading towards the gate, and by that time the fire crew had managed to move the Land

Rover so there was a gap wide enough for the ponies to run through and make their escape to open countryside.

The twins were horrified.

'They'll get out,' said Harry.

'Not if I can help it,' said Charlotte, spinning round and running towards the fire engine.

'Charlotte!' yelled Harry. 'What are you doing?'

In seconds she was climbing onto the fire engine. She opened the door and scrambled inside the cab.

Over by the Land Rover, the crew commander glanced up and saw her.

'Oy! Come out of there!' he shouted and raced over to stop her. But, before he could, Charlotte had punched the red button on the dashboard and suddenly the deafening noise of the siren sounded over the field. The ponies were alarmed by the terrible din and stopped suddenly in their tracks, digging their hooves into the soft ground.

Butterworth, unable to hang on, went shooting over Bonnie's head like a guided missile and landed in a muddy heap with the breath knocked out of him.

Boyle, on the other hand, managed to cling onto Rio a while longer until the Welsh cob reared up and tipped him off so that he slid into a mound of horse manure the brothers had been saving to put on their allotment.

The firemen abandoned the car, ran over to the bedraggled men and hoisted them to their feet.

'They're criminals,' said Harry, walking beside the crew commander. 'Now do you believe us? Why would they try to get away if they weren't up to something?'

Before the fireman had time to answer, they heard the sound they had been hoping to hear. The wail and yelp siren of a Lothian and Borders Police car. It was heading their way.

'About time, too,' said Charlotte. 'Now we'll see some action.'

Two white Vauxhall Astras with blue and white Battenberg markers on the side came screaming up the main road, strobe lights flashing, and swung onto the track that led to the monastery. The first screeched to a halt close to the fire engine and two policemen leaped out while the second car pulled up behind and two more officers appeared.

'Are there only four of you?' said the crew commander.

'Afraid so,' said the policeman. 'But we are the best.'

'Then see what you make of this lot,' he said,

pointing to Boyle, Butterworth and Ivan Sikorsky. But before the police could begin their interviews, there was a dull whirring noise overhead.

'A police helicopter!' yelled Harry. 'Fantastic! I've only seen those on TV.'

Charlotte nodded. 'Now we've got our very own cop show.'

As they gazed up into the moonlit sky, an EC-120 Colibri came through the clouds and into view, hovering over the field before beginning its descent. This light, single-engine helicopter was known as the Hummingbird, and had nothing – absolutely nothing – to do with the police.

43
The Hummingbird

All eyes were focused on the helicopter as its nose-mounted searchlight lit up the field. It was attempting to land, but twenty terrified pigs and two startled ponies were running free across the grass and making it impossible. If it landed on any of these large animals, it would be tipped off-balance and its rotor blades would smash into the ground. So, instead of trying to touch down, it hovered fifteen metres above the field.

The police officers questioning Ivan Sikorsky were distracted by the spectacle and the Russian took the opportunity to catch them off-guard. He balled his fist and struck out, first one and then the other, knocking them off balance onto the grass. Then he spun round and fled across the field, followed by Edina – mud-splattered and barefoot. The helicopter was their means of escape.

When Harry realized what was happening he yelled, 'They're getting away!' But a policeman grabbed his arm to prevent him from running after Sikorsky.

He watched, helpless, as the doors at the side of the Hummingbird slid open and a rope with a harness on the end was lowered to the ground. The Russian and Edina ran with their heads bent forward, blasted by the wind from the rotor blades, until they finally reached the dangling rope. Sikorsky grabbed the harness and slipped two straps over his shoulder and pulled two more between his legs before fastening the locking device over his stomach. He signalled to the pilot to winch him up.

'What about me?' screamed Edina above the noise of the helicopter.

As Sikorsky's feet lifted off the ground, he looked down at her and his one-finger signal was coarse and obvious. He intended to leave her behind.

But Edina Ross would not be abandoned and she flung her arms round his legs.

It was too much for Harry. He struggled and wriggled until he slipped out of the officer's grasp and raced across the field. By the time he reached the helicopter, Edina Ross had already begun to lift off the ground as she gripped hold of Ivan Sikorsky's legs.

She was almost two metres off the ground when Harry arrived. He leaped up and managed to grab hold of her feet. She screamed and kicked frantically, trying to dislodge him whilst holding on to Sikorsky. But she couldn't shake him off. Harry was like a limpet. He would not let go even when he felt his feet leave the ground. Would he be able to hold on? he wondered. And for how long?

But suddenly strong hands gripped his ankles. He looked down and saw LOVE HATE. Where had he come from?

'If you think you're going without me,' he yelled, 'you've got another think coming!' His huge body hung onto Harry's legs and this extra weight meant that the helicopter failed to lift off. And when four police and several firemen joined them and grabbed hold of LOVE HATE, the weight of all those bodies made it impossible for it to fly away.

Sikorsky looked down at the long line of people and shouted at them to let go. But the noise of the engine and the rotor blades was deafening. He shouted again before reaching into his jacket and pulling out his Glock semi-automatic pistol. Buffeted by the wind, he pointed it at Edina, securing his aim. Then he fired.

A few millimetres to the right and it would have hit her. But the shock alone made Edina Ross let go and she fell, her mouth open in a perpetual scream, until she landed on Harry, trapping the others below in a mangled heap of arms and legs.

With her hair wild and tousled and her clothes streaked with mud, she leaned forward, staring at Harry, her eyes crazed with fury. While the mass of bodies beneath them struggled to free themselves, Edina grabbed Harry by the throat and shook him.

'Leave me alone,' he gasped but the air was choked out of him and the words were little more than a croak. He struggled and tried to free himself but he felt like a rag doll in her powerful hands. Move, move, Harry said to himself. But it was no good. She was on top of him and he couldn't. The blood was racing round his brain, his pulse was pounding until he felt as if his head would explode. Then everything went black as he lost consciousness.

The police, preoccupied with a frantic struggle with LOVE HATE as he tried to escape, failed to notice Harry's predicament. It was Charlotte who came to his rescue. 'Hang on, Harry,' she yelled as she ran across the field.

'You!' Edina screeched as she saw her clambering over the heap of bodies.

'Yes, me,' said Charlotte and grabbed a handful of Edina's hair. 'Sorry to spoil your hairdo.'

She yanked. She tugged. She almost tore the hair out by its roots, so that Edina screamed and released her grip on Harry's throat. She clapped her hands to her head and that was when Charlotte pushed her off-balance and sent her tumbling down onto the grass gasping for air.

When the police and the firemen finally struggled to their feet, they found Charlotte sitting on top of Edina. And there she stayed until they had secured her hands with a pair of very uncomfortable handcuffs.

44
Home Again

After interviews with the police, they were home again – Dad, Harry and Charlotte – and things felt almost normal. Of course, there would be more in the days to come. But, for now, they were home.

They arrived back in the early hours of the morning and crashed out until almost eleven o'clock the following day. It was only then that they noticed the light on the answerphone was flashing. There was a message from Mum.

'My darlings,' she said, 'I've been ringing all day. Where are you? I'm on my way back earlier than I thought. Isn't that wonderful? I hope things haven't been too dull for you, Harry and Charlotte. I expect Dad's been taking you out to some nice places. Anyway, I'm dying to tell you all about Hollywood and I should be back sometime on Friday afternoon. Don't worry, I'll get a taxi from the airport. See you soon.'

They had only a few hours before Mum arrived and she wouldn't be impressed to see the mess the flat was in. Harry and Charlotte hadn't done a perfect job on clearing up after the break-in. So they tidied rooms as best they could, packing things into drawers, running the vacuum cleaner over the carpets and loading the dishwasher with dirty cups and plates. And, by the time the doorbell rang soon after two o'clock, they had finished.

Mum was there with two suitcases and several parcels, smiling broadly – until she spotted the bruises on Dad's face.

'What on earth . . .?' she said, reaching up to touch his cheek.

Dad grinned sheepishly. 'It's nothing,' he said. 'Just a knock.' Then Mum flung her arms round Harry and Charlotte and almost squeezed the breath out of them.

'Have you managed without me?' she said. 'The flat looks very tidy, I must say.'

Dad winked at the twins and they grinned.

'What's the joke?' she asked.

'Come into the kitchen,' said Dad. 'I'll make some coffee and we'll tell you what's been happening.'

They sat round the table, biscuit tin in the middle, and Harry and Charlotte told their astonished mother the whole story of how Dad was kidnapped by Ivan Sikorsky's men and how they found him in the monastery.

'I'm horrified,' she said. 'Tell me you're making it up.'

'We're not,' said Harry, taking a HobNob out of the tin. 'We just wanted to find Dad. And when we found that reliquary with the diamonds we knew it had something to do with his disappearance.'

Mum turned to look at Dad. 'You'd better explain about this reliquary, James. What happened?'

Dad ran his hand over his forehead and sighed. 'I borrowed it from the museum,' he explained. 'Edina Ross works there. Except she was in London on the day I collected it.'

'Edina's that old university friend of yours, isn't she?'

'Friend!' Charlotte interrupted. 'No way.'

'Right,' said Dad. 'But I didn't know that at the time. When I found the false bottom in the reliquary and those *diamonds* . . . well, I just rang her on her mobile. I thought she needed to know as soon as possible.'

'What did she say?' Mum asked.

'She must have been in the conference. Her mobile was switched off – so I left a message explaining what had happened.'

'And did she get back to you?' asked Mum.

'It turned out that she was working with a crook called Ivan Sikorsky. She rang him instead and told him to get the reliquary back as soon as possible. He decided a burglary would be the best way. After all, if the reliquary had disappeared, there was no way I could prove to the police that I'd found diamonds in it, was there?'

'So Edina was involved in some kind of scam,' said Mum. 'Illegal diamonds, I presume?'

'Yes,' said Dad. 'She always did like living the high life and travelling round the world.'

Mum was confused. 'But James,' she said, 'why did they kidnap you?'

'When they didn't find the reliquary in the flat, they took me to Sikorsky's hideout in a monastery and tried to make me tell them where it was. Two stupid men beat me up so badly that I couldn't speak, even if I'd wanted to.'

'Oh, my goodness,' said Mum, clapping her hands to her cheeks. 'People like that! They could have killed you.'

She felt sick at the thought of James in so much danger. She pulled out a tissue, blew her nose and wiped her eyes. She couldn't believe what she was hearing.

But Charlotte was eager to tell more. 'Harry and me found the reliquary after they'd kidnapped Dad.'

Mum flopped back in her chair. Her mouth open. She didn't think she could be any more surprised. But she was wrong. Charlotte told her the whole story.

'You see,' said Harry, 'Sikorsky was ex-KGB and he'd stolen a load of relics during his time in Russia. He managed to create false bottoms in some. That's where he hid the diamonds. The police told us.'

'But why was the museum involved?' Mum asked.

'Because Edina Ross could sell to customers abroad,' Harry explained. 'It was a good cover. Respectable and all that. It was really easy to export the diamonds.'

'It was just tough luck that Miss Calder let Dad borrow one of her 'special' relics. It was part of a new consignment,' said Charlotte, 'and Edina would never have let that happen if she'd been there.'

Mum poured herself another cup of coffee. Her head was whirling with all the amazing things the twins were telling her. She poured milk into the cup and sat down again.

'And – guess what?' Harry continued. 'We saw Sicko smuggling the diamonds. Honest, Mum. We watched them come in by boat. They had guns and everything. We hid behind a rock and saw the criminals . . .'

She held up her hands. 'Stop! Stop! I can't bear to hear any more. These people are so violent.' Then she wrapped her arms round Harry and Charlotte and hugged them close. 'I am very proud of my brave children but please promise me you will never do anything like that again.'

Harry wriggled free and grinned before he took another biscuit.

'Did you know, Mum,' said Charlotte, 'you could carry a million pounds' worth of diamonds in your pocket? That's why Sicko put them into the reliquary. It was such a simple thing to do.'

'They were blood diamonds from some part of Africa,' Harry explained as he munched on the biscuit. 'They were being sold to pay for weapons, the police said.'

'It's illegal to buy them, you know,' said Charlotte. 'Only crooks like Sicko would do it and he made loads of money.'

'Enough!' said Mum, standing up and waving her arms. 'Let's have a break and I'll show you what I've got.' She fetched the presents she had brought back from the States and handed them out. There were books about Hollywood for Dad, and for Charlotte and Harry there were two battery-powered scooters. One silver and one red.

'Cool!' said Harry.

'Foot-operated power switch!' said Charlotte. 'Fantastic!'

Mum laughed. 'After all your excitement, they must seem rather tame.'

Not a bit of it. The twins zotted down the hall, then from one room to another at top speed, making loud whooping noises, endangering the potted plants and the glass vases. When they finally knocked over a small table in the hall, Dad told them to stop.

They all went into the living room and settled on the sofas.

'What happened to Ivan Sikorsky?' Mum asked. 'Did he escape?'

Harry nodded. 'He's probably on the other side of the world. But the police will track him down,' said Harry. 'They found Father Abbot, you know. He was tied up in one of the bedrooms.'

'And they found our bikes,' said Charlotte. 'The reliquary was still in the saddlebag after all that time.'

'And my bike was still leaning on the railings,' said Harry. 'I couldn't believe it hadn't been nicked.'

'Marvellous,' said Mum. 'It's nice to know there are honest people in the world.'

The phone rang. Dad picked it up and walked into the hall to answer it.

When he returned he said, 'That was my publishers. They wanted to know if I've decided on the design for the book cover.'

'Well, I don't suppose you want that reliquary on the front now, Dad!' said Harry.

'Nope,' said Dad. 'Too many terrible memories.'

Charlotte tapped her chin. 'The book's called *Medieval Murder,* isn't it?'

'Yes.'

'Then, how about a photograph of a crook dressed up as a monk?'

'I don't suppose you were thinking of a Russian by the name of Sikorsky, were you?'

And they all laughed.

45
Havana, Cuba

Ivan Sikorsky lay on the flea-ridden mattress, naked except for blue striped underpants. Sweat rolled down his forehead and dripped off his chin. The hotel room was small and hot and every surface was covered in a thick, yellow dust. Although a fan rotated above the bed, it failed to cool him. It only stirred the sticky midday heat.

That morning, the Russian had been met at the airport, as arranged, by Diego Banos, a small and powerfully built man of twenty-five with jet-black hair, a tanned skin and white teeth interspersed with gold. Sikorsky followed him out of the airport building and climbed into a battered, rust-covered Ford which was waiting to take him to the Hotel Manolo.

Diego drove with wild abandonment down the narrow streets of the old town, narrowly missing people walking from the market.

'Good hotel,' Diego said, pulling up at the kerb side. 'My grandmother's hotel. You like?'

Sikorsky did not like – but it was just for a few

hours, he thought. It was good enough. He reached into the pocket of his jacket and handed Diego one small diamond.

'There will be more when you come back,' said Sikorsky.

Diego nodded. 'Of course. I fix boat for you. We go tonight across to American coast. We go in dark, you understand?'

In the hotel room, Sikorsky stripped off his clothes and flung them onto a broken chair. Even the strap of his Rolex felt hot on his wrist and he took it off. Then he flopped down on the bed and lay there, his enormous stomach rising and falling in the heat, covered with the grease of sweat. In spite of the disgusting room in which he found himself, he was pleased. He smiled with satisfaction as he remembered how he had escaped the police and had had the presence of mind to take the diamonds with him. False passports, identity papers and flights to Havana were expensive. But still, everything had gone smoothly. In a few hours he would be in America, ready to set up a new business.

A new life.

He spread out on the bed, scratching his belly to ease the fleabites. Exhausted after the long flight, his eyelids soon grew heavy in the airless room and he fell into a long, deep sleep. When he woke, daylight had faded, cockroaches were out of their holes, skittering across the floor, and he felt mosquitoes feeding on his naked skin.

He sat up, brushing the insects away, wondering what had happened to Diego Banos. Surely he should be here by now. He flicked on the light switch and reached for his watch to check the time.

But the watch was not there.

Frantically, he looked around the room, under the bed, behind the chair. It was gone. Someone had taken it while he was asleep. His beautiful, expensive Rolex Oyster had been stolen.

He had hardly grown used to this catastrophe when he suddenly remembered his jacket. Panic-stricken, he grabbed it off the chair and felt in the pockets. They were empty. No diamonds. No passport. No identity papers.

He roared with rage. 'Aaaaagh!' He flung the door open and tore down the wooden stairs, stumbling as he went.

At the bottom stood the owner of the hotel. Consuela Fernandez Garcia. A fierce woman of sixty dressed from head to foot in black with greasy hair drawn back from her face.

'Robbed! I've been robbed,' yelled Sikorsky, not caring that he was naked apart from underpants.

The old woman narrowed her eyes and shrugged. He suddenly realized that she had had the perfect opportunity to steal. Who else could have slipped into his room and taken the watch and the diamonds?

'You!' he yelled. 'You took my things while I was asleep.' He raised his hands to hit her.

'I have sent for the police, señor,' she said, facing up to him with her arms folded across her chest. 'They are right outside.'

Then, to his surprise, Consuela Fernandez Garcia began to scream with an intensity that shocked Sikorsky so that he clapped his hands over his ears. She was still screaming when the door burst open and four uniformed police ran into the hotel and grabbed him.

The conversation that followed was in rapid Spanish of which Sikorsky understood not one single word. But it ended with his being handcuffed, taken to the local prison and dumped in a cell with three fearsome men who hadn't washed for weeks. Compared with this cell, the Hotel Manolo was a palace.

Ivan Sikorsky had no money and no passport. But worse than that, he soon learned that the law in Cuba could be very slow to react. For instance, the case of a man charged with attacking a defenceless old woman could take years to come to court.

Years and years and years.